THE DARK

FRANCIS KING was born in Switze. [...] in India before being sent back to En[...] [...]ight student, he earned a Classics scholars. [...]xford, but later changed to English literature, and [...]st novel, *To the Dark Tower* (1946) while still an undergra[...] [...]is novel, and his next two, *Never Again* (1947) (an autobiographic[...] novel based on his childhood) and *An Air That Kills* (1948), were published by Home and Van Thal, which then went bankrupt, but not before King had established himself as a promising young novelist.

Beginning in 1949, King worked for the British Council and travelled extensively, including to Italy, Greece, and Japan, all of which would provide settings for his novels. His next book, *The Dividing Stream* (1951), set in Florence, won the Somerset Maugham Award and cemented King's status as one of the bright young literary stars of his generation. During the 1950s and 60s, King published a string of excellent works, including *The Dark Glasses* (1954), *The Man on the Rock* (1957), *The Widow* (1957), *The Custom House* (1961), and *The Waves Behind the Boat* (1965).

In 1966, King resigned from the British Council to devote himself to writing full-time and supplemented his income by writing book and theatre reviews and working as a literary adviser to the publishing house of Weidenfeld & Nicolson. He continued to write prolifically, and notable highlights include the gay-themed novel *A Domestic Animal* (1970), which drew a threat of a libel suit, *The Action* (1978), which narrowly missed the Booker shortlist, and *Act of Darkness* (1983), which, unlike many of King's books—which were usually well-received critically—was relatively successful commercially.

King went on writing until his death in 2011, making the Booker longlist with *The Nick of Time* (2003) and publishing a revised 60th anniversary edition of *An Air That Kills* with Valancourt Books in 2008; his final novel, *Cold Snap*, appeared in 2010.

JONATHAN FRYER (b. 1950) is a British writer, broadcaster, lecturer and Liberal Democrat politician. His books include biographies of Christopher Isherwood and Dylan Thomas and *André & Oscar*, about the literary friendship of André Gide and Oscar Wilde. He lives in London.

Cover: The cover is a reproduction of the jacket art from the 1954 first edition, published by Longmans, Green and Co.

By Francis King

To the Dark Tower (1946)★
Never Again (1947)★
An Air That Kills (1948)★
The Dividing Stream (1951)★
The Dark Glasses (1954)★
The Firewalkers (1956)
The Widow (1957)
The Man on the Rock (1957)★
So Hurt and Humiliated, and Other Stories (1959)
The Custom House (1961)
The Japanese Umbrella, and Other Stories (1964)
The Last of the Pleasure Gardens (1965)
The Waves Behind the Boat (1967)
The Brighton Belle, and Other Stories (1968)
A Domestic Animal (1970)
Flights (1973)
A Game of Patience (1974)
The Needle (1975)
Hard Feelings and Other Stories (1976)
Danny Hill: Memoirs of a Prominent Gentleman (1977)
The Action (1978)
Indirect Method and Other Stories (1980)
Act of Darkness (1983)
Voices in an Empty Room (1984)
One is a Wanderer: Selected Stories (1985)
Frozen Music (1987)
The Woman Who Was God (1988)
Punishments (1989)
Visiting Cards (1990)
Secret Lives (1991)
The Ant Colony (1991)
Yesterday Came Suddenly: An Autobiography (1993)
The One and Only (1994)
Ash on an Old Man's Sleeve (1996)
A Hand at the Shutter (1996)
Dead Letters (1997)
Prodigies (2001)
The Nick of Time (2003)
The Sunlight on the Garden: Stories (2005)
With My Little Eye (2007)
Cold Snap (2010)

★ Available from Valancourt Books

FRANCIS KING

THE DARK GLASSES

With a new introduction by

JONATHAN FRYER

VALANCOURT BOOKS

The Dark Glasses by Francis King
First published London: Longmans, Green and Co., 1954
First Valancourt Books edition 2013

Copyright © 1954 by Francis King
Introduction © 2013 by Jonathan Fryer

The right of Francis King to be identified as Author of this work has been asserted by him in accordance with the Copyright, Designs and Patents Act 1988.

Published by Valancourt Books, Richmond, Virginia
Publisher & Editor: James D. Jenkins
20th Century Series Editor: Simon Stern, University of Toronto
http://www.valancourtbooks.com

Library of Congress Cataloging-in-Publication Data

King, Francis, 1923-2011.
  The dark glasses / by Francis King ; with a new introduction by Jonathan Fryer. – First Valancourt Books edition.
     pages ; cm. – (20th century series)
  ISBN 978-1-939140-19-7 (acid-free paper)
  I. Title.
PR6061.I45D37 2013
823'.914–DC23

                              2013014355

Set in Dante MT 11/13.5

INTRODUCTION

MANY of Francis King's close friends—including myself—were intrigued by the apparent disconnect between his own sweet nature and the unpleasantness of so many of his fictional characters. The simple truth was that he was fascinated by people with blatant flaws—people who lied or cheated or stole, or behaved badly in some other way. This was not the sexual attraction for the criminal felt by a Jean Genet or a Francis Bacon but rather the satisfaction of intellectual curiosity. He was asking himself in wonderment: how could they possibly act that way? What makes them tick? It sometimes exasperated those of us who loved Francis how tolerant he was of friends and acquaintances who were clearly dishonest, arrogant or outrageously selfish, but these were the sort of people he liked to observe as a novelist, hungry for material, rather as an entomologist might examine a particularly exotic specimen under a microscope.

There is no out-and-out monster in *The Dark Glasses*, but the novel offers a cavalcade of unsavoury characters, misfits and dysfunctional relationships. The (anti-)hero Patrick Orde, an English botanist and amateur photographer of independent means, is fascinated but also at times revolted by the uninhibited passions and actions of the peasantry on the island of Corfu, where he and his anglicised Greek wife, Iris, have moved to try living on her family's small estate. On arrival he has a dreadful premonition, though he is not quite sure of what. A modern Greek tragedy then unfolds, as his attention is caught by a sweating 15-year-old peasant girl working in the fields and her slightly older brother, both of whose fates will eventually be sealed by Patrick's presence.

As winter turns to spring and the Corfu sunlight intensifies, Patrick dons the dark glasses of the book's title. These effectively protect him from the increasing glare of the cruel and dangerous reality around him. The metaphor of the sunglasses is developed further when his first pair of dark glasses goes missing and he buys a replacement with reflective lenses that prevent anyone seeing his eyes and by extension therefore knowing what he is thinking. The glasses act as a barrier that reinforces the separation between the worlds of the privileged foreigner and the "primitive" locals. Moreover, in Patrick's case the inability to see, understand and communicate properly seems to characterize all his relationships, including those with his wife and her overbearing mother.

Francis usually drew inspiration for his characters and the location of his plots from real life. This had disastrous consequences in one later instance, when the former British Labour Member of Parliament, Tom Skeffington Lodge, recognised himself in the caricature of a snobbish Brighton landlady in what I have always considered to be Francis's finest novel, A Domestic Animal, and threatened to sue. Francis had to sell his own beautiful house in Brighton to raise the money to pay an out-of-court settlement to get the case dropped and the original edition of the book was withdrawn. There was no such disastrous fallout from The Dark Glasses, mercifully, though the Greek woman to whom the book is dedicated, Marie Aspioti (who ran the British Council Institute on Corfu), did later reject Francis as a friend after they had a blazing row about the justification or otherwise of Greek Cypriots using terror tactics to get rid of the British colonialists from Cyprus.

Francis spent several months on Corfu in 1952, as part of a year's subsidised literary activity funded by the Somerset Maugham annual travel award for young writers. Maugham intended the award to enable the beneficiary to travel abroad to find new inspiration for their work. The 29-year-old Francis's case was unusual in that he had already had several novels published and was actually living abroad, working for the UK's cultural diplomacy arm, the British Council, in the Greek capital, Athens. However, Maugham agreed that Francis could use the money to take a year's unpaid leave of absence from his job and stay on Corfu to work on a new book.

When Francis was there, Corfu was still an undeveloped part of one of the poorest countries in Post-War Europe, which had moreover been devastated by Nazi German occupation, followed by a vicious civil war. Apart from the British Consul and his family and his children's governess there was only one other English person on the island: an attractive young woman married to a Greek (the reverse of the Patrick and Iris Orde situation in the novel). Francis stayed in the Pension Suisse, then the one and only hotel on the island, located on Corfu town's main square. Through the cold winter months he stayed in his room, which was heated by a log fire, putting in a full day's work on a novel. In the evenings he was often entertained by Marie Aspioti in her large but somewhat run-down house and he managed to find time to write articles, poems and reviews for the magazine she edited for the Institute as a way of thanking her for her hospitality.

When the novel he was working on was finished Francis realised it was not very good, so he binned it. He then set to work on another book, which many years later he described in his autobiography, *Yesterday Came Suddenly*, as his *roman-à-clef: The Firewalkers*. It is presented as a memoir and contains explicit passages about the coming of age of a young Englishman abroad and the colourful characters he encounters. Unfortunately, according to British Council rules all employees who wrote a book (which they were in fact encouraged to do) had to submit it for approval by the Council's headquarters in London before it could be published. The homosexual elements to *The Firewalkers* were considered so scandalous by the British Council's senior officials—homosexual activity between even consenting adults in private being illegal in Britain until 1967—that Francis was informed that he would either have to resign from the British Council if he wanted to have the book published under his own name or else he must use a pseudonym. He wisely chose the latter course, inventing the name Frank Cauldwell for the authorship of his book, and thus kept his job. The critics hailed this "Mr. Cauldwell" as an interesting new talent and the book sold well.

The final months of his Maugham Award year Francis spent in London seeing family and friends but also working on a third book: the short novel that would become *The Dark Glasses*. He was able to draw on his recent experiences on Corfu to use the island as its setting and he probed two areas of the human condition that would be central to all of his writing life: sexual attraction and bad behaviour. In contrast to the openly gay characters in *The Fire-walkers*, the homosexual element in the plot of *The Dark Glasses* is subliminal. It is not only Patrick who fails to pick up the signals until the very end, but also all but the most perspicacious reader.

Casual homosexual encounters were very much part of the life of young Greek males at that time, when girls were unavailable except through marriage. Christopher Isherwood gives a memorable portrayal of the rampant and guiltless promiscuity of Greek island boys in his fictionalized volume of autobiography *Down There on a Visit* (published in 1962). Soldiers in particular were often on the lookout for a foreign gay man who might offer them a meal or cigarettes or some other small gift in exchange for sexual favours. Francis was by no means the only expatriate to take full advantage of that availability. But he also made many real friends among the servicemen he met in cheap *tavernas* in the poorer neighbourhoods of Athens and elsewhere in Greece. It was with them that he first tried pot, for example.

Sixty years on, for those of us living in an American or European environment in which homosexuality has become largely accepted by the mainstream of society (even to the point of the legalisation of equal marriage in some states and countries) aspects of the life enjoyed—or sometimes more accurately endured—by gay men before homosexuality's decriminalization can appear shocking, even distasteful. There was often a commercial transaction involved and the encounters were usually between a middle class man and a poor working class or peasant youth. Class was still very much a feature of life in 1950s Europe, and the class distinctions come over very strongly in *The Dark Glasses*. Moreover a peasant or servant girl as young as fifteen (as Soula is in the novel) would often in that period have been considered "fair game" by many men. Francis was no socialist—in fact, he was a paid-up member of Britain's Conservative Party for most of his life—but he disliked the way some people who considered themselves "better" than others treated labourers and servants. That comes over very clearly in the cameo role of Patrick Orde's mother-in-law. It would be wrong to draw the conclusion from the unflattering portrayal of Mrs. Nicolidou, or indeed of Iris Orde, that Francis was a misogynist, however. On the contrary, he adored women, including his sisters and mother, in a purely platonic way of course; a majority of his friends were women.

Style and language have changed greatly since 1952, which means that *The Dark Glasses* does have a distinct period feel to it, though there is no harm in that. At times the writer comes across to the modern reader as precious in his turns of phrase, whereas in fact Francis was acknowledged as a master of beautiful and precise language. Some individual expressions may jar or seem odd today; in particular, the term "nigger brown" might shock, even appear racist. But 60 years ago this was indeed a recognised colour in textile manufacturers' catalogues, especially popular for making secondary school girls' uniforms. Francis was the very opposite of a racist, displaying a deep and intelligent interest in peoples and cultures from around the world, especially the Middle East and North Africa.

Even though the novel was written quickly, Francis was proud of *The Dark Glasses* and was disappointed when it received scant praise. I suspect that was partly because on first reading the novel's subtle messages can be easily missed. Like some films, which reveal deep new layers when watched a second time, a second reading of this book reaps rich rewards. I actually think it is one of Francis's best books, so I am delighted it is being republished.

JONATHAN FRYER
London

April 9, 2013

THE DARK GLASSES

To
MARIE ASPIOTI
in love and gratitude

1

AUTUMN

I

"THERE is something amiss with the younger people here in Corfu, though I find it hard to explain what. You'll discover that for yourself soon enough," Mrs. Nicolidou said, continuing to address her son-in-law, as she had done throughout their drive, and to disregard her daughter.

But Iris now asked: "How amiss, mother? What do you mean?"

"I mean——" the old lady bounced up and down in a cloud of dust and the words were choked in her. "Careful, careful, Christo!" she exclaimed irritably in Greek to the young man at the wheel of the dilapidated Rolls-Royce, speaking his name with the French r-sound that always made other Greeks assume that she was a foreigner.

"Sorry," the young man muttered. "But with the road like this, what can I do? And the car needs new springs."

A hysterical cackling and squawking merged with the groans of the engine as they swung round a corner.

"What on earth is that?" Iris asked.

"The two cockerels that Frangoudis gave me."

"Are they alive?" Patrick asked. "Where are they?"

"They're on the luggage-thing behind. I hope Christo tied them on firmly. . . . Christo——" one of Mrs. Nicolidou's beautiful hands, weighted with its encrustation of old-fashioned rings, was extended to his shoulder—"there's no chance of those birds getting loose, is there?"

Christo shook his head, but the old woman's hand remained on his shoulder for several seconds afterwards, in that casual physical intimacy so common even between superiors and inferiors in Greece and so rare in England.

"What was I saying?" She clawed away a sticky strand of white hair from her forehead with the fingers that had rested on the man's soiled shirt.

"This heat—it's extraordinary for late autumn! . . . Ah, yes— that there was something amiss with the young people here. The old people are very much what they always were, but with the younger people one feels that the salt has lost its savour. They have no vitality, no real interest, no resources from which to draw. They're apathetic. It's not like that in the rest of Greece—perhaps we here are beginning to pay the price of over-civilization. Nobody *does* anything. Is it the effect of the war? Or the climate? Or poverty? Or unemployment? Really I don't know. When you go to the Club—as of course you will do, sooner or later—you'll meet a lot of quite agreeable young men playing canasta or ping-pong. But ask who is So-and-so or So-and-so, and you'll always get the same answer: 'Son of a rich father.' In my day, young men didn't sit around waiting for things to happen. And it isn't like that only in the town. Even in the villages . . ."

Iris was turning over the pages of a pre-war magazine which she had found rumpled at the bottom of the car.

"Isn't it odd," she cut in, in her deep, toneless voice, "here's the copy of *Vogue* from which I got the idea of my wedding-dress. It must have lain here all these years." Patrick leant over from his tip-up seat to examine the glossy picture upside-down. "You remember I took it to Madame Alexandra, and then I must have stuffed it in here and forgotten all about it. How hideous it looks now," she added.

"You looked very pretty in it," her mother said firmly. "Didn't she, Patrick?"

Patrick, who had turned to gaze down from the window at a glittering oval hundreds of feet below them, merely asked: "What's that? Is it a lake, or part of the sea?"

But nobody answered him. Iris continued to stare at the photograph of her wedding-dress, the magazine resting across her broad knees, and her hands, large and white and shapely as her mother's, tucked under her in an oddly childish fashion; while Mrs. Nicolidou leant forward to chide Christo: "You've never fixed that strut of the hood. Really, it's quite impossible. I've told you and told and told you."

The glare from the distant water was making Patrick's eyes ache, and he drew some dark glasses from his pocket, murmuring: "That's better," as he opened them and raised them to his face. Now the silver oval deepened to green while the whole landscape of jagged rocks, laboriously terraced vineyards and dazzling sky relaxed; expanded; lost its flatness, hardness and clarity. A mysterious veil descended; even the noise of the car and the chatter of the two women seemed to grow muffled.

Patrick sighed. All at once he had experienced a sensation of almost melancholy calm, combined with a vague premonition, he could not have said of what.

They were passing a church, its white-washed holy-of-holies bulging askew, and Iris, who was looking out of the opposite window, crossed herself hurriedly, as peasant-women do, once for each member of the Trinity.

"Why did you do that?" her mother asked sharply. Iris did not reply. "What an extraordinary thing to do! So it's true that you've become a *religieuse*."

The face of the daughter, oddly defenceless in spite of its large-featured impassivity, twitched as it always did when some emotion struggled upwards to express itself.

There was more hysterical squawking as the car swerved to avoid a lorry.

"I can't bear to think of those wretched creatures behind," Patrick said. He pulled off his glasses and then shut his eyes. "Is it really necessary for them to suffer like that? Is it?"

But he had again asked a question to which neither of the two women would give him an answer.

·   ·   ·   ·   ·

It had never before struck Patrick that his wife was like her mother. But as she directed Christo and two helpers where to place the luggage, her voice seemed to take on the same authoritative edge and her hands the same authoritative gestures. It surprised Patrick that after eleven years she should return home, to the

house that was now hers, with so slight a show of emotion. Some
of the peasant-women were crying as they embraced and kissed
her on either cheek, but Iris's only response was a kind of subdued irritation, until, suddenly breaking free from them, she leapt
up the steps in twos and threes and disappeared into the house.
Patrick himself had been touched by the shrill cries of welcome
that had sounded so much like cries of lamentation; by the eagerly
grasping hands; and by the tears themselves that had rolled, large
and facile, down the women's dark-brown, crumpled cheeks.

"The house is a beauty," he said, following his wife: to do so, he
had had to drag his hand away from an old woman who was rubbing it between both her own with a sensation as of pumice-stone
on his skin.

Iris did not answer; she was shouting at Christo who was lurch-
ing behind her, a trunk on his shoulders, and then she turned to
one of the other men, pointing out a room with what was almost
a dramatic sweep of her firm, white arm. Habitually her gestures
were anxious and tentative. Now she was having some altercation
with Christo in Greek, turning from it to explain to Patrick: "He's
made a mess of my instructions. I said you wanted this room as
your dressing-room, and he's fitted up that."

Patrick glanced in turn through the doors of the two rooms and
then, because he felt sorry for the man, sweating and breathless
under his burden, he said: "Oh, but he's quite right. I much prefer
the room that he's given me." He ventured on the first words
of Greek he had spoken for eleven years. "Thank you, Christo. I
approve of your choice."

"As you wish," Iris said. "Careful! Careful! Don't throw the
trunk down like that! Oh, and this shutter seems to be broken.
But, Christo, I told you to make sure that everything was in order.
How careless you've been!"

Christo stood leaning against the headpiece of the bed, a lean
hand massaging one of the brass balls with which it was orna-
mented. He must be less strong than he appeared and he was out
of breath, his chest rising and falling under his khaki shirt, his
mouth open and his nostrils distended, as he gasped for air; his
thin face, with its immeasurably sombre eyes, had become a dirty

grey. He cleared his throat and began to excuse his omission, but Iris said: "Oh, never mind! See what has been going on outside, would you?"

He licked his lips and swayed slightly against the bed as he gazed first at her and then at Patrick: until, all at once slapping the brass ball with the palm of his hand so that it twirled round and round, he loped from the room.

Patrick leant out of the window; then he drew back as he realized that in the courtyard below a number of faces, male and female, were upturned to stare at him.

"Oh, this inefficiency is maddening!" Iris exclaimed. "I'd forgotten what it was like. There's no paper in the drawers, and this one has got some mouldy potatoes in it. Potatoes! I do think mother might have given the place a look over."

"But what are you complaining about? I think it's absolutely charming. Look at these flowers—" Patrick pointed to a chipped enamel jug in which some roses had been arranged—"that was kind of someone. Do you think Christo sees to that? He, or his sister? . . . Christo, did you put these here for us?" The man had returned. Setting down another two boxes—one contained Patrick's photographic equipment, another his microscope—he wiped his forehead with the back of his hand as he said: "I hope you didn't mind."

There was a curious similarity, Patrick realized with a shock, between the man's deep toneless voice and Iris's.

"Mind? Why on earth should we?"

Iris said grimly: "And what about the hot-water bottles in the bed, Christo?"

"They've been in all day. Anna"—this was his sister—"is just refilling them."

"I can't understand why mother insisted on going home instead of coming to give us a hand. I suppose she wanted her tea. She's one of the greediest people I know. . . . No, Christo—no, no, no! Mr. Orde's typewriter is to go in the study."

When the man had left the room, Patrick turned from the window to say gently: "Don't talk to them like that. It doesn't suit you."

"What do you mean?" At once, all this new, and to him distasteful, air of authority crumbled away from her.

"He seems a decent chap," he said. "They all seem decent. So why shout at them?"

"I wasn't shouting. You—you don't understand . . ." Once again that odd twitch passed over her features, usually so impassive in their regularity: she was colouring slowly—a thing she rarely did. "Anyway, what did I say? What did I do that I shouldn't have done?", she got out in a fluster.

"Come!" he said. He drew her to the window and put an arm round her shoulder. "Isn't it beautiful?" Below the house was the courtyard, and below the courtyard the small white-washed church; below the church itself the village tumbled away into odd ravines, sloping scraps of field sewn together by erratic footpaths, and dry gulleys full of white circular stones the size of cannon-balls. Everywhere there were trees heavy with oranges. He had drawn her closer as a voice said in Greek in the doorway:

"Sorry, sir."

"Come in, Christo. Come in!"

But the man had already vanished; and Iris had jerked away as if the contact of their two bodies was in some way illicit and shameful.

"How agreeable this all is!"

Iris said nothing.

"Isn't it, my dear?" One of Patrick's small, neat black shoes slipped on a stone and he went "Whoops!" as, clutching at a bush, he managed to save himself from falling backwards. "I don't think I've ever seen anything quite so beautiful."

Yet, even at that moment, he was conscious that this hillside, dimming in the light of evening, with its white houses, its orange-trees and its crooked, stony paths, suffered, in some way he could not explain, from its own impeccability. There was nothing lacking, nothing to be improved: and this very perfection of form and colour and light induced a feeling first of elation but then of satiety and even boredom.

"I hope you're not going to be too cold," Patrick said a moment later, when Iris still remained silent.

She tucked the ends of her tartan stole into her belt: "Soon it will be cold," she said. "In a week or two it'll be impossible to go out in the evenings—mark my words."

They had left the village and there closed about them a heavy, constricting silence in which the noise of their feet scrabbling over the gleaming white stones sounded oddly loud. In the distance goat-bells were tinkling.

When they passed the derelict chapel which they had already passed in the car, Iris said:

"One moment. . . . Do you want to come in?"

"No, I don't think so."

She pushed intrepidly through the nettles round the entrance and the door creaked behind her. Patrick balanced himself on a rock, his knees almost touching his chin, and took out a cigarette. He felt a vague distaste whenever she gave evidence of this religious trend of hers and though he would like to have seen inside the chapel, he had deliberately refused to go with her out of a wish to express that distaste in however oblique or futile a manner. After their only child had been stillborn, Iris had more and more immersed herself in what Patrick could only regard as an absurd and unattractive faith; but though they had sometimes discussed religion together, they had never discussed religion as it affected him or her—conversation with Iris was almost always in general terms.

With a shrug of the shoulders, Patrick had let her go her own way, as he let most people and things go their own way. How profound was this religious emotion? What lack or unhappiness did it appease? To what extent was it drawing her further and further from him? His mind would grip each of those questions momentarily and then, as though afflicted by some kind of intellectual cramp, would at once let them slip. She must go her own way. . . . And he would turn, as he always turned, this middle-aged man detached to the point of selfishness in his chosen serenity, away from these problems to his violin-playing, his botany, his photography, his collection of Cretan ikons; just as now he turned away from the disagreeable thought of his wife, on her knees in the murk of that nettle-choked, bat-haunted ruin of a chapel, and

began, with a kind of voluptuous elation, to note the scenery
about him: the extraordinary gradations of colour from sapphire
to indian ink, except where a throbbing bar of orange rested
across the horizon below or an olive-tree glimmered, a vague puff
of mist; the sudden declivities, the gentle knolls, the squat white
houses, from which the lamps had begun to gleam; and then the
lake, like a bronze-coloured bubble resting on the narrow stone
causeway that thrust between it and the sea. How beautiful it was!

The goat-bells tinkled closer: under some trees he could see the
glimmer of white pelts, and then (breathing out the smoke of his
cigarette as he rested his chin on his palm) he made out a human
form. A chain rattled and the form—boy or girl, he could not yet
see—sneezed loudly. Suddenly in that curious dimming light what
had been so indistinct a moment ago could be discerned with the
utmost clarity. It was a youth who stood, out of the shadows of
the trees now, with his large hands hanging clumsily to his sides
and his face gleaming like a white smudge out of the greenish twi-
light. The goats had been let go, and from time to time there was
a tinkle of their bells as they skipped from one tuft or hillock to
another.

The boy was probably fifteen or sixteen, and he was wearing
an old Army blouse and some heavily-patched Army trousers
tucked into boots that were grotesquely large for him. There was
something savage and animal-like about his slouching stance, his
enormous hands, and the mat of coarse hair that fell in a tangled
fringe across his forehead. Patrick could not see his eyes, but he
was sure that they were fixed on him.

The boy took something out of his pocket and moved back
among the trees. It was a jack-knife, and he opened it with a
clumsy deliberation, his head bent down, and then began to hurl it
again and again at a tree, with such force that he had to tug it out
of the bark after each throw. It seemed such a pointless exercise
at that hour, in that light, and Patrick wondered if it was intended
as a display for his benefit. But while thus absorbed the boy never
once looked in the Englishman's direction; he seemed to be wholly
absorbed in the actions of hurling the knife, retrieving it and hurling it again.

Iris came out: "Sorry to have kept you waiting."

"What's it like inside?"

"Gone to rack and ruin. It would be fun to rebuild it. Shall we walk on, or turn back?"

"Oh, let's walk on."

As they continued down the path, Patrick wanted to look round to see if the boy was staring after them: he could no longer hear the plock-plock-plock as the knife pierced the wood. But something prevented him. It seemed to him strange that Iris had either failed to notice the boy or, having noticed him, had made no comment.

"That's mother's house—over there."

"Oh—as near as that?" Lights gleamed out of a shallow wooded trough. "Shall we look in on her?"

"No."

He laughed. "How odd you are—both of you, I mean. English people behave like that when they haven't seen each other for eleven years, but not Greeks, I thought."

"What do you know about Greeks?" It was curious how, after being married to her for more than a decade, he could still never be certain what moods lay submerged under that monotonously flat diction.

"Hang it all. I've lived in the country."

"I didn't ask you what you knew about Greece—that's something different. Of course you have the reputation of knowing more about the flora of Greece and the Balkans than anyone else living. I hadn't forgotten that."

So he had been right to suspect an irony.

When they reached the causeway, he asked: "Shall we walk out?"

"It'll be windy. But, yes, let's try."

On the left was the lake, glimmering in lunar repose; on the right the choppy sea, fretting against the causeway, so that as they walked a light spray settled on their hair, their faces and Iris's bare arms.

From the lake came a smell fishy and sour; from the sea a biting tang.

"The fish move from the sea into the lake—under here they

go—and then they can be easily netted." Three lines, one purple for a boat, one black for its fisherman, and one grey and wavering for the pole which he grasped, made a triangle on the copperish sheen of the lake. The man shouted a greeting at Iris when he saw who she was, and she waved back. "That's Dino—Christo's elder brother," she explained to Patrick. "He rents the fishing rights on the lake from us."

"Is the lake yours?"

"Ours," she said. "Yours and mine."

When they reached the other side of the causeway Patrick was delighted to find an orchid, growing on the hillside, which he had seen only once before.

He gazed for a long time at the four stiff petals, curling back, eggshell blue spattered with gold, and then handed it to Iris. She put it to her nose:

"Thank you. But"—she grimaced—"what a horrible smell!"

"Horrible?"

She tucked the flower into her belt and walked on without saying anything more.

They returned home in silence, the neat, small Englishman with his youthfully unlined face under close-cut grey hair stumbling beside his wife who, magnificent in her strength and stature, strode out sure-footed along the rocky path. When they reached the village, it was already almost dark. Two mongrel dogs, the bones protruding through their mangy coats, circled each other, capering and snarling from time to time in a pretence of enmity, before the door of a hovel from which ivy dripped like hair. A woman's voice, clear and nasal, was singing from behind a wall. In the only tavern in the village old men in cloth caps and tattered Army greatcoats dyed black stared bemusedly at backgammon boards, or flung down playing-cards worn by use into greasy octagonals.

Someone was working at a patch of ground near Iris's house, striking the ground blow after blow with a pick-like implement. Patrick thought at first that it was a man, but when they came closer, he realized it was a girl. When she heard the scrunch of their footsteps, she stopped and turned and leaning on her implement surveyed them as they passed. She was bare-footed and appeared to be wearing nothing but a tattered mud-coloured frock, rent under the arm so that part of an immature breast was visible, white against the brown. Her arms and neck were massively strong, her dishevelled hair tawny.

"Soula!" Iris called.

The girl merely stared at her.

"Don't you remember me? *Kyria* Iris—*Kyria* Orde, now. I used to take you paddling."

The girl came towards them with a curious sideways walk, as if she were afraid that one of them might suddenly spring at her to attack her. When she was about three feet away, she made an abrupt movement of the right arm, catching Iris's hand in hers and, with a kind of bobbing curtsy, pressing it to her lips. Iris said with a dreamy detachment: "How nice to see you again! It was clever of me to recognize you after all these years, wasn't it? You must be fifteen now."

The girl's eyes, large and frightened as some wild animal's which has only just begun to make friends with its captors, darted from Iris to Patrick and then back to Iris again.

"This is my husband," Iris said. "I expect you've heard about him."

The girl merely stared at Patrick: and under that gaze, sombre and frightened, he found that he himself was shrinking away.

"It's very late to be working," Iris said.

But the girl was already returning to her pick, till once again she was hurling it at the soil, her hair falling tangled across one cheek, in a savage rhythm punctuated by occasional grunts and gasps of effort.

"How they work!" Iris said. "These poor women! And her father must be the richest man in the village. You remember—he shouted to us from the lake . . . What's that?" she started. "Oh, it must be her brother. . . . Hello, is that you, Stavro?"

A figure was leaning against a post in the same pocket-handkerchief of a field where the girl was working.

"Yes," a voice answered. "Who is it?"

"Iris Nicolidou—you remember me, don't you?"

It was, Patrick realized, the same boy whom he had seen with

the goats outside the ruined chapel; but, unlike his sister, he made
no effort to come forward to greet them.

"Yes, I remember you," he said. "Hello." His voice, immature
yet deep with a rustic slurring of the consonants, seemed to carry
with it a faint tang of insolence.

Then, as they walked on, he began to sing softly:

> *"Après la guerre finie*
> *Soldat anglais parti*
> *Chaque demoiselle a piccaninny . . ."*

"Why isn't he digging that bit of ground, instead of his sister?"
Iris demanded angrily. "Oh, it depresses me so! In two or three
years' time she'll be given away to some clod-hopper with a dowry
of a hundred gold sovereigns, a dozen olive-trees and perhaps an
odd cow or two. In ten years she'll be unrecognizable—worn out
by work and childbirth. Greeks are right to talk about going to
'Europe' when they go abroad; we are not yet a European people.
There are so many things I hate about my own country. I'd forgotten what misery there was!" For a moment disgust and anger
churned the placid surface of her composure; then they subsided
and all was again monotonously flat and still.

"And isn't there misery enough in England?" he asked. "I doubt
if there's any more here."

She gave a brief, contemptuous chuckle.

"Why do you laugh like that?"

"You know so little about misery," she said.

"What do you mean by that?"

"It's true enough, isn't it? I don't say it in criticism. You have a
knack for extracting what is valuable from the garbage-heap, and
leaving the rest—without even getting your fingers soiled." Again
she gave that deep, contemptuous chuckle. "I envy you that."

"Well, I suppose both of us have been more than usually fortunate in life," he said equably. Then, changing the subject, as he
always did when they seemed to be entering on to ground where
their effortless progression together might suddenly be checked,
he said: "I wonder what Christo's sister has got us for supper. I'm
hungry, aren't you?"

"Yes, very fortunate," she muttered in an echo of what he had said before.

Christo served the meal to them, moving silently in the shadows round the long, narrow table at either end of which they found themselves placed. They ate a soup of egg and lemon, and then roast kid, cooked with garlic. Eventually Iris began to ask Christo about the estate for which he had acted as bailiff during her years abroad and he would pause as he moved about at his tasks and answer in that monotonously flat, quiet voice that was so much like her own. It seemed odd to Patrick not only that she should maintain towards the man always that same air of cool authority but also that he should not resent it; for Mrs. Nicolidou had told them with what courage and cunning Christo had saved the property from the depredations of the Germans during the war, of how he had risked his life over and over again for her, and of his innumerable kindnesses to her when her income from her Indian and Egyptian investments no longer reached her. He had lent the old woman money; he had even fed her at a time of famine. Yet Iris never for one moment relaxed that attitude of superior to inferior, never for one moment made even the briefest acknowledgment of the debt the family owed him.

When Christo went out to fetch some fruit, Patrick said: "There's obviously no point in my trying to run the estate. Even without his percentage as bailiff, I'm sure we'd make only half as much if I bungled everything."

"But I thought the idea was to give you something to do."

"Oh, I shall find a great deal to occupy me."

Christo came back; and now as he stooped over the table, with a bowl of oranges in his hands, his bony, saturnine face with its long, slightly hooked nose, heavy eyebrows and darkly gleaming eyes, was illuminated momentarily by the lamp. Glancing up, Patrick experienced an extraordinary stab of pity. Perhaps it had been merely some chance juxtaposition of shadows and highlights, but he thought he had never seen an expression of such indescribable despair and suffering on a human face.

After dinner, Iris said that she would do some unpacking, and Christo offered to help them.

"I don't know if there's much you can do. Unless, of course, you begin to uncrate that box with the silver in it."

"Christo must be tired," Patrick said in Greek. "Let's leave it till tomorrow."

"No, I'm not at all tired; really not at all tired."

"You've done enough for one day," Patrick said. "Thank you, Christo—thank you for everything. Have you eaten?"

"Not yet."

"Then go and eat."

"But I'm not hungry."

"Of course you are hungry. Go and eat." As Christo went out into the kitchen, Patrick said: "I like him so much."

Iris did not reply.

They unpacked some books together and then they sat down, on either side of the open hearth in which some logs were blazing. Christo had been told earlier by Iris that it had been wasteful of him to light the fire on such a warm evening, but now a chill had begun to creep through the old rambling house with its vaulted ceilings and ill-fitting doors, and they were both glad of the flames. Patrick lit his pipe. He ought to be tired, he told himself, after the journey by boat from Athens and the excitement of their arrival; but though he leant his head backwards against the chair and closed his eyes as if in a deliberate attempt to woo that expected tiredness, it obstinately would not come. He sighed, shifted uneasily and kicked out at a log so that sparks whirled upwards. Iris was staring into the heart of the fire, her large white hands resting on the two wooden claws of her chair, and her face impassive yet vaguely troubled under its coiled mass of hair.

Patrick got up: "I think I shall go out for a stroll. Coming?"

"*Another* stroll?"

"Yes—why not? I've eaten too much. I feel I need some exercise."

"No, I shall finish off this box."

He walked down the deserted lane to the tavern, but although it was barely half-past nine, the customers had all left and the proprietor, a middle-aged man with short, bandy legs and a port-wine stain on one side of his face, was swabbing the tables before locking up. He knew who Patrick was, and beckoned him in eagerly

as he stood, shy and hesitant, in the doorway. They talked of England, a country which the other man, like so many Greeks, seemed
to regard as an earthly paradise, and then of the unemployment
and poverty of Corfu: but even this last topic could not curb the
Greek's exuberance or joviality. He had poured Patrick a large
tumbler of red wine, and now he asked him whether he liked it.
The flavour was acrid as vinegar, but out of politeness Patrick said
that yes, the wine was excellent.

"Of course it's excellent! It's made from Madame's grapes!"
The man roared with laughter, stuck out his legs and massaged his
crutch with one hand as with the other he raised his glass to his lips
to drain it to the end.

It was only later that Patrick realized that by "Madame" he, of
course, meant Iris.

There seemed to be a slight frost in the air when Patrick left the
tavern, stumbling a little over the unmade road and feeling light-
headed after his three tumblers of wine. Everywhere there was
silence until, as he climbed up the path to the house, he heard
something rustle in a tree above him. He thought it must be a cat,
that dark shadow which merged with the shadows of the leaves.
But as he walked on, he heard:

> "*Apres la guerre finie*
> *Soldat anglais parti . . .*"

The voice was hoarsely unmusical, mocking, almost sinister.

Christo was clearing up the paper and straw from the box they
had unpacked, when Patrick re-entered the house.

"Has my wife gone to bed?"

"Yes."

"You should go to bed too."

The man said nothing.

"Leave that until tomorrow. It really doesn't matter."

Suddenly Patrick noticed that, in the buttonhole of his shabby
blue-serge jacket, Christo was wearing the orchid he had picked
that evening for Iris; and even as he glanced at it, the Greek
coloured and said:

"I hope you don't mind my taking this. The *Kyria* had thrown it into the hearth."

"No, of course not. Have it, please." Patrick watched Christo for a while as he continued to sweep up the rubbish. Then he said: "Your nephew was out when I came back from the tavern."

"My nephew?"

"Isn't that your nephew—your brother's son?"

"Oh, Stavro—yes." Christo picked up an armful of paper. "He's not a good boy, I am afraid, sir," he said as he walked out to the kitchen.

He had disappeared before Patrick could ask him what he meant.

2

PATRICK had grown used to looking out of his study window after breakfast, as he read the air-mail edition of *The Times*, and seeing the queue of peasants, some squatting morosely on the garden wall, some chatting in groups in the roadway, while they waited for Iris. He noticed that the women and men rarely mixed together, and that a man always took precedence over a woman, however late his arrival. Often the queue would remain until after midday, so that when Patrick went out for a walk he would have to weave his way between tight, black-clothed groups who would invariably get up for him, the men touching their caps and the older women drawing a scarf or placing a hand over their faces. Massed together, a curious smell clung to them: an odour, not unpleasant, as of damp soil.

Sometimes Patrick would go down, out of curiosity, into the room where Iris worked. She wore a white linen coat, changed each day, with her hair invisible under a white gauze napkin, and as he stood in the doorway, watching her at her work, she was usually too absorbed to notice his presence. If she did notice him, she would merely give him a preoccupied "Hello" and tell him to hand her something—a bottle of penicillin, a syringe or a bandage. The silent stoicism, no less than the terror of these peasants when confronted by illness, touched him unbearably. He had never once heard a cry or complaint, even the children allowing an abscess to be lanced or a wound to be probed with what seemed to be a trance-like fortitude. Yet when they suffered even the most trivial ailment, they would give way to despair: pleading with Iris to make them well, to fix them up somehow so that they could work, and not—not, they would entreat her—to pack them off to hospital where they would die under the surgeon's knife. Many of them, Mrs. Nicolidou said, perhaps in exaggeration, had never been naked since the day they were born: and often they would stubbornly refuse to show their bodies, expecting Iris to prescribe for them without any further examination of the pains of which they talked. They suffered a terrible ignominy, above all the men, when they sat shivering under Iris's direct, impersonal gaze.

Patrick told her that she was overworking herself; and combined with an admiration for the fanaticism with which she tended her patients, he would, from time to time, experience a strange pang of jealousy. He had never been jealous of her before. She had become thinner and paler and often when he talked to her at meals or in the evening, she would answer with a vague preoccupation and then get up, a moment later, to scribble some note to the surgeon in Corfu, to go out to give an injection, or to see if Christo's sister, Anna, had prepared the invalid food for some sick old woman dying alone. Each day more and more people seemed to be gathered outside the house; for Iris's fame had begun to spread to the other villages. "Really I do so little for them," she would often protest. "I feed them, get them clean and make them go to bed—that's about all. Fortunately most illnesses are self-remedying." She was wonderfully efficient, wonderfully calm, wonderfully confident of her own ability to cope with emergencies as formidable as a severed artery or glass in a child's eye; and yet—this, to Patrick, was always slightly repellent—he had never once seen her show pity or horror or affection in the face of the miseries of those she tended. Of course, he would tell himself, that impersonality was essential to any doctor or nurse; and yet, he could not say why, her attitude disturbed him and filled him with exasperation.

One such morning when he had gone to watch her at work

had been particularly difficult for her. A peasant from a neigh-
bouring village had arrived with all the symptoms of appendicitis,
but when Iris urged him to go to the hospital in Corfu—she even
offered to have him driven in their car—he had stubbornly refused,
demanding over and over again to be given "that medicine you
gave my cousin". Although it was a cold November day, the sweat
ran down his broad, ruddy face and trickled on to the hair that
sprouted from his open-necked collar, as he kept doggedly insist-
ing. The medicine turned out to be castor-oil, and Iris explained
that it would be dangerous to give him a laxative in his condition.
But by now he was maddened by terror and pain, and he began to
shout that it was wickedly unfair; that she refused him the medicine because he came from another village; that for all she cared,
he could go off to the hospital and die there—die in agony. He
thumped on the table so that instruments rattled in a basin and his
dog, which he had tied to a chair-leg, leapt up and barked, dragging the chair with it. Well, so be it! He'd leave them! he shouted.
But they'd be sorry! They'd be sorry! He rushed out, pushing his
way violently between the people gathered around the door. Iris
dropped her hands to her sides; for a moment she looked utterly
defeated. Then she went out and spoke to an old man, urging him
to fetch the peasant back. She returned, her brows drawn tight,
and looking up, for the first time noticed Patrick: "Hello! Did you
hear all that?"

"Yes."

"How stupid they all are! One gets tired of trying to help them.
And that wretched dog has gone and made a puddle." She shouted
to a youth at the head of the queue, and threw a cloth at him: "Do
me a favour—wipe up that mess. Then I'll see to you."

Patrick sat down and continued to watch as, one by one, the
peasants came in. Sometimes Iris would murmur a comment to
him. Once she said brutally: "This poor wretch will be lucky if he
survives the winter—both lungs are gone"; once with a biting exasperation: "They can't even tell you where anything hurts. They
just know they have a pain, that's all. Do you mind this stench? I've
long since got used to it."

Suddenly there was a sound of a violent altercation in the passage outside. Patrick supposed that it must be the peasant with the dog who had returned. "Take your turn!" a woman shrieked, and then a man shouted: "Let them in! Go on, let them in!" The door was burst open, and as Iris demanded sternly: "What does all this mean?" all the excited, angry voices rumbled into silence.

There were two girls; one Soula, Christo's niece, and the other a gipsy in a ragged orange skirt, reaching to her feet, a no less ragged and soiled blouse of purple silk and a quantity of metal jewellery. The gipsy, who seemed no more than a child, was clutching a bundle to her with hands on which the nails grew like talons that had been scratching in the earth.

Soula came forward: "This girl's baby is very ill. I met her in the road. She has walked all the way from Pelakas to see you. I said I would bring her to you."

"She should have waited her turn."

"But the baby is very ill."

"Tell her to sit down. I must finish this dressing."

Soula tried to get the girl to sit in a chair, but she preferred to crouch, in one corner, her legs crossed as she rocked the bundle back and forth, back and forth, crooning softly as she did so. Soula leant against the wall, her bare feet together and her bare arms, on which the hair shone golden in a shaft of late autumn sunshine, crossed before her while she stared down to the ground. She was wearing the same dress she had worn on the first evening, but Patrick noticed that the rent under the arm had now been patched. Her toes were short and widely spaced from always walking bare-foot; her legs were lean and muscular as a boy's. Patrick felt strangely moved by her animal-like beauty, her air of submission, and the latent savagery which he detected, however erroneously, beneath that submission. Once she looked up, and realized he was staring at her: and the muscles in her magnificent throat contracted momentarily before she looked down again.

"Now," Iris said.

The gipsy girl got up and laid the bundle on the table. She sniffed, rubbed the back of her soiled hand across her nose, and wiped the hand on her skirt. Iris unrolled the bundle. There was silence; then she said:

"But this child is dead!"

The girl let out an extraordinary wail.

"It's quite cold. It must have been dead for hours."

The girl threw herself on the floor, she clutched Iris's legs, screaming: "Save it! Save it! Save it!"

Iris said: "I tell you, it's dead."

But the girl continued to clutch at her, screaming:

"No, no, no! Save it! No! Save it! Give it your medicine!"

The tears welled out of her eyes and streaked down her cheeks, her whole body shuddered and writhed, and from time to time she would drum with her feet on the floor like a child in a tantrum.

"Be quiet!" Iris said. "The baby is dead. Get up. Get up, I tell you." Suddenly she leant forward, and Patrick thought she was going to caress the girl; but instead she slapped her across the face. "Get up," she repeated.

The girl gasped; Soula ran forward and put her arms about her. Quietly now the girl sobbed on Soula's breast, while Soula murmured inaudibly to comfort her, running her short, stubby fingers over the other's greasy and tangled hair.

"Take her into the kitchen, Soula, and tell Anna to feed her. If she won't eat, at any rate make her drink something. Find out where she's from, whether she's married. She may need some money. I'll come and see her later. All right, take her away now!"

Iris wrapped up the dead baby again in its pathetic covering of rag, brown paper and a strip of grey blanket, and then carried it into the ante-room where she stored her medicines. There seemed to Patrick an appalling callousness in the matter-of-fact way in which she had dealt with the situation, and he felt the desire to make some protest to her. But while he was summoning the courage to do so she had come out to the table where the baby had lain, sat slowly down in the straight-backed chair, put her arms on the table, and then, all at once, rested her face sideways on her arms with the long exhalation that one hears when someone faints. But she had not fainted; her eyes were open, staring at the wall.

She remained like that for a few seconds; then she shook herself, pulled her white jacket straight and got up and strode to the door. "Who's next now?" she asked. "Don't push—don't push! Get back to your places!"

Later Soula returned. She stood silently leaning against the door until Iris glanced at her; then she said: "We can't do anything with her. She's lying on the floor of the kitchen. She won't get up. We've tried to feed her and make her drink."

"Then leave her. She'll get over it in a few hours." In English she said to Patrick: "They're fortunate—their grief works itself out in a single wild paroxysm. What's the betting in a week she'll have forgotten the whole business? . . . Hand me that syringe, would you?" She turned back to Soula.

"Hand you what, *Kyria*?"

"The needle-thing in the basin there."

Soula hesitated and then picked up the syringe as though it were an unexploded bomb. She went and stood beside Iris, watching her intently as she filled it with penicillin: the young boy whom she was going to inject was lying on the couch, his face buried in the pillow and his hands clenched at his sides, in silent terror.

"What's it for?" Soula asked.

Iris explained in detail: Patrick had expected her to make a brusque retort, as she usually did when the peasants questioned her about the treatments.

"Can't I help?" Soula ventured when Iris was later doing a fomentation.

"Yes, you can. But you'll have to wash those hands of yours."

Soula looked down at them.

"And tie up all that hair. . . . Here, take this carbolic soap, and this nail-brush—scrub really hard. Then put on this jacket and this cap."

Soula went out into the kitchen as Iris said to Patrick: "I need an assistant. She seems a sensible type of girl. I might be able to make something of her."

Normally Patrick did not remain for more than five or ten minutes when he visited Iris at her work: but now curiosity, mingled with another emotion which he had not yet acknowledged, kept him in the room. At first Soula was clumsy and hesitant; but it was remarkable how soon she learnt what Iris had to teach her.

She seemed to have a natural gentleness which calmed the worst terrors of those who arrived for treatment. "I think you've made a good choice of assistant," Patrick said in English.

"Yes, I've had my eye on her for some time."

After Soula had been helping Iris for the best part of an hour, her father came in. Unlike his lean, sombre brother he was a jovial, plump man with curly hair, a red face which became purple after he had drunk a couple of glasses of wine, and a deep bass laugh. He had spent some years in America, and he usually wore a wide-brimmed brown borsolino on the back of his head and chewed at a cheroot.

"Hello, hello, hello," he said. "So this is where she is! I've been ransacking the place for her." He went up and put a large hand, the back of which was covered in reddish hair, on to Soula's shoulder; at the contact the girl seemed to stiffen, although she did not move away.

"Yes, Soula has been helping me. She's an excellent assistant."

"That's a good girl!" Her father squeezed her shoulder, and then gave his rumbling laugh: "But how are we going to manage for cabbage in the winter, if Soula doesn't plant them?"

Soula, who had so far kept her gaze fixed on the linoleum, now gave her father a brief, shying glance as she wriggled under the hand which still lay heavily on her. Then she looked across at Iris.

Iris at once said: "I hope you don't mind my taking her like this. Of course I shall—shall make it up to her for the hours she gives me."

"Well, that's very kind of you! I'm sure she'll be glad of a little pocket-money—won't you, Soula? But it's not really necessary. You know us folk here, Kyria Iris, we're poor, but we have our *philotimo.* . . . Well"—he touched the brim of his hat with a blunt forefinger—"I must take myself off. When you've finished here, Soula, you'd better skip down to Mile End field and see if the goats are all right." He once again gave his jovial laugh as he left them: "I never thought they'd make a nurse of you," he said.

Not many minutes afterwards Christo appeared, carrying a box of medical supplies that had been sent out from the hospital. Saying nothing, he crossed the room from one door to the other and went into the ante-room. "You'd never believe they were brothers, would you?" Patrick said.

When Christo had gone, Iris said: "He's not well. I'm sure he's not well."

"What makes you think that?"

"Well, look at him! And he's worried about it too. . . . Soula, what's wrong with your uncle?"

"Wrong with him?"

"Does he feel all right?"

"Well, he complains about this pain of his. But he's always made a fuss about his health."

"What pain?"

Soula shrugged her shoulders. "He says he gets a pain, I don't know where."

"I thought there was something wrong. I knew it. . . . He'd better see Petropoulos when he drives that appendicitis patient down to the hospital."

"But Christo won't see a doctor!" Soula exclaimed.

"He'll have to," Iris said grimly. "I'll see to that."

That night, when they lay side by side in bed, Iris suddenly said: "I hope there's nothing seriously wrong with Christo."

"Why should there be?"

"Petropoulos says he must have an X-ray. Now I suppose I'll have another struggle to get him to go for it." She sat up in bed, leaning on her elbow, with her uncoiled hair falling about her.

"It's merely a routine, I imagine," Patrick said.

Iris sighed: "We can't afford to lose him." She added: "He's indispensable to us."

"No one is indispensable. . . . But why should we lose him?"

Patrick felt vaguely strung-up. They had made love, some ten minutes ago, but he had experienced none of the hoped-for relaxation. He was restless, tense, vaguely dissatisfied, he could not say why. Perhaps it had been the suspicion—one which often now came to him—that Iris submitted to him not from pleasure or even a desire to give him pleasure, but from no more than a futile sense of duty. On such occasions she would never protest; and really, he asked himself, what grounds had he for having this suspicion? None, none at all. How often he had looked into her face, seeking some vestige of disgust or humiliation, and had found there only that usual impassivity. Yet tonight the suspicion nagged on and on. Greek girls were trained in a code of complete obedience to their men; it was what, not only their parents, but also their Church enjoined upon them. The men did what they wished; the women-folk submitted. Yes, but Iris had long since ceased to be a Greek! She was Europeanized. . . . Then he remembered how, driving up in the car, she had crossed herself at that chapel, once for each member of the Trinity, as he had seen the peasant-women do.

He threw the end of their top blanket away from him: "It's so hot!" he exclaimed. "Do you mind if I open the other half of the window?"

"No, open it."

After he had fixed the catch, he remained looking down, past the moonlit courtyard, past the savage hillside with its ravines that looked like cracks fretted by acid in steel, past the mirror-like bur-nish of the lake, past the causeway, out towards the sea. Was it an illusion that the wind brought with it a tang of its salt? And was it the distant waves, or merely the blood in his ears, that he could hear whisper and thud? He felt a curious easing of his tension, as though key after key was being turned in invisible locks or knot-ted muscles were relaxing gently under the strongly persuasive hands of a masseur. How beautiful Corfu was, he thought—as he thought so many times each day. It must be the most beau-tiful place in the world: he had used that phrase in his letters. He thought momentarily of his years in his father's business, jagged pieces of that other life scraping together in the recesses of memory: tedious dinner-parties for clients; the antagonism of his brothers; stifling conventions of dress; his unpunctuality and incompetence and hatred of the whole dazzling edifice on which his family's wealth was founded. . . . Out of it—out of it at last! He wanted to burst out laughing with that sudden exaltation.

"Don't catch cold."

"No, I shan't catch cold."

He stood, his arms extended to either side of the window,

and the wind flapped the loose collar of his pyjamas and ruffled through his hair. The lake was like an enormous eye covered by the gleaming silver-grey gristle of a cataract; the sea heaved and plunged and seemed to thunder louder and louder in his ears.

When at last he went back to bed, Iris was still leaning on her elbow, the flesh of her arm gleaming with a wonderful subdued radiance through the mass of tumbled jet hair. As he stretched himself beside her, she felt for his hand; her fingers were icy.

"How awful the world is!" Suddenly, with that same exhalation she had given as she had returned from depositing the gipsy's bundle in the ante-room, she rested her forehead on his shoulder. Momentarily she shivered, and her hands tightened their grip: "The baby . . . I can't stop thinking of the baby."

He wondered if she meant her own, or the gipsy's, and as he did so, he realized that through all the weeks they had spent on the island he had never for one second thought of the child, their child, which, had it lived, would now be nine years old.

3

Mrs. Nicolidou was angry.

"This arrangement is really far from convenient. Iris should have remembered it was the night of the Club dance and have consulted me first. I don't at all like to bring the Baroness so far out of her way. Surely it would have made no difference if Christo had gone into hospital a day later, would it?"

Patrick was astonished by her selfishness. "Petropoulos takes the view that he ought to operate as soon as he possibly can."

"Yes, but a day! A day can't make any difference! . . . If it were anyone but the Baroness, I wouldn't mind so much. Iris had no right to ask her before consulting me. I don't like the woman— it's common knowledge she was spying for the Germans for years before the war—and I don't like to put myself under an obligation to her. Apart from the fact that that station-wagon of hers is very far from comfortable. . . . Anyway, is Christo so ill? He looked quite fit to me."

"Very ill."

"I'm afraid he's one of those people who give way too easily. He's always been like that."

"It's difficult to do anything but give way to cancer," Patrick said quietly.

"Cancer!" They had been wandering through the garden, Mrs. Nicolidou ahead of Patrick, because of the narrowness of the path, with one of her white, heavily-ringed hands drawing up the wide pink-and-grey skirt of the French eighteenth-century costume she was to wear to the dance. Now she turned round, terrified and appalled. "But who said anything about cancer? I never heard anything about it. What nonsense! Did Petropoulos say . . . ?"

"That's what he told Iris."

"She never told me." She snapped off a twig from a tree beside her: it was a Japanese orange, and the small, hard fruits swayed like gold nuggets in the late autumn sunshine; Patrick almost expected to hear a tinkle. "She never said anything to me about—about cancer." It obviously cost her an effort to bring out the word.

"Well, that, apparently, is what it is."

She walked rustling on, to turn again after a few moments: "This has quite spoiled my evening." She spoke as if she were blaming him. "I'm no longer in the mood. I don't feel I can go."

"But of course you must go."

"Is Iris very upset?"

"Upset? What about?"

"About—about this unfortunate thing of Christo's."

"Naturally we're both awfully upset. He's such a thoroughly decent chap. We don't know how we shall manage without him. It's amazing how much he does."

"Who's going to take his place while he's in hospital?"

"Dino, his brother."

Mrs. Nicolidou sniffed. "Unwise," she said.

"Unwise? Why?"

She shrugged her shoulders: "He's not another Christo."

"He seems capable—and amiable."

"Oh, he's that all right. But you'll have to watch him. He's never been a favourite of mine. And that wife of his, before she married him she was personal maid to Lady Perrott—Perrott, you know, was our last ambassador but three—and it seems to have given her the idea that she's several cuts above the rest of the village people. . . . Oh, well!"

She sighed: "I didn't really expect Iris to consult me before making a decision of that kind. But let it go on record—I think she's made a mistake." They had now completed a wide circle back to the verandah, and Mrs. Nicolidou said: "Come in and have a drink. I feel I need something before I face the Baroness."

She herself mixed the dry Martinis and rattled the ice energetically inside the cocktail-mixer, as she remarked: "It's silly of you and Iris not to come to this dance. It's quite the most amusing of the season. And besides—you'd meet such a lot of people. You've been here seven weeks, isn't it, and you've hardly met a soul. Did something go wrong that time you went to the Club?"

Patrick smiled: "No, of course not. It was really quite enjoyable. But we just don't feel it's worth that long drive to spend an evening playing ping-pong or bridge—or dancing."

"Oh, heavens—you are a dull pair! Do you know how old I am? Sixty-nine. And I haven't missed one of the Saturday night dances since my Athens jaunt. You can't just vegetate here."

"Oh, I admit I vegetate—and I enjoy vegetating. But that word can hardly be applied to Iris."

"This mania of hers for prayer and good works! . . . Let me give you another of those." She reached for the cocktail-shaker. "She's always been far too serious—but now she's carrying it beyond a joke. Don't you agree?"

"No, really I admire her enormously for what she is doing . . ."

"Oh yes, I suppose it is wonderful!" There was a suppressed rancour in the old woman's voice; obviously, Patrick thought, she envied her daughter for the affection and respect she had won so rapidly from the villagers. "But it's also a little absurd, really. It's not as if they were grateful . . ."

"Of course they're grateful."

"Greek gratitude! That never lasts long. Look how they talk about you English and the Americans—after all you've done for them. One would imagine that everything wrong in the country could be ascribed to English or American misdeeds. No, we're a proud people here—and gratitude and pride are never easy bedfellows. . . . That's the car, isn't it? I think I can hear it turn up the hill. Can't you?"

Patrick could hear nothing: obviously the old woman's ears were far sharper than his.

"How do I look?" She fluttered her fan, pirouetted round and then made him a deep curtsy, as a young girl might do, with all the high spirits, nervousness and suppressed excitement of her first ball.

"Marvellous," he said: it was no more than the truth. He noticed how smooth and white was the skin of her bare throat and arms; how brilliant her eyes under the strong, arched brows; with what litheness and grace she moved. Then he imagined to himself how gauche and self-conscious Iris would be in the same situation, even her shoulders flushed by her embarrassment and the fan trembling between her large fingers. It was cruel to make that comparison between the two women, he told himself as soon as he had made it; and he felt a profound shame.

"Heavens!" Mrs. Nicolidou was looking out of the window. "Do peep at the Baroness! What is she meant to be! Is she wearing a turban on her head—or a tea-cosy?" The bell rang. "That's the Albanian chauffeur who's said to be her lover. . . . Well—" she began to gather up her things—"I do wish you young people were coming with me. It's awfully silly of you."

It was a long time since Patrick had thought of himself and Iris as "young people".

4

IRIS had for some time been complaining of the room which she called her "surgery"; it was small and badly lit, and, tucked as it was between kitchen and dining-room, it was inconveniently placed. She had looked around for a substitute, and had eventually decided on one of the store-rooms which covered the whole ground-floor of the house. The advantage of this store-room was not merely its size but also the fact that it was provided with a separate entrance of its own.

When she told Christo of her plan, he had said that the room was at present used by Soula and her brother, Stavro, as a "den"—Patrick had been amused by the word, the same in Greek as in English; it had seemed so apt when applied to the hideout of those two savage children—but that, of course, they could be ordered to quit as soon as Iris wished.

"I plan to have the builders in on Monday—there's a lot that must be done. I want you to go into Corfu this afternoon and find a sink for me. There are also some other things I shall need." She spoke, as she always seemed to speak to Christo, with a curious hectoring edge to her voice and he, as always, received each of her instructions in silent humility. Christo's attitude seemed to Patrick quite as distasteful as Iris's: he would have liked the other man to answer her back, to contradict her, and to assert his claims on her gratitude and respect.

In the event the buying of the sink, the white enamel paint and a hospital cupboard were the last commissions that Christo performed. By the next Monday he had already undergone his operation.

Patrick had not been able to sleep on the night after he had waited in the hospital for five hours while Christo was on the table, and early the next morning, as he lay still awake, listening to the peasants going to work in the chill November dawn—there were no voices, only the tramp of boots, the tinkle of goat-bells and the clatter and scrabble of donkeys' hoofs on stone—he had decided to go for a walk. Silently he got up, and drew on his clothes over limbs that were stiff and aching with fatigue. He left Iris asleep, her cheek pillowed on the curve of one firm, white arm.

Slowly, the dawn greyness quickened: and the faces which he passed, set in apparently immutable lines of weariness, grimness or despair, seemed to quicken with it, as did his own spirits. Just as his mind would always let go of any stubborn problem, so now it let go of Christo and his illness, that piece of unresolved grit that had inflamed it through the long hours of night. Nothing was resolved; all was released. . . . Once more the pattern was repeated; once more he experienced an illusory liberation into a world full of beauty, light and joy.

When he returned, three-quarters of an hour later for breakfast, a small crowd was gathered in the courtyard of the house: there were three builders, in overalls stained with whitewash, Iris, Soula, Dino, and a number of other villagers, women and men. The Greeks were all gesticulating and shouting at each other simultaneously, until Iris quelled them: "Oh, shut up, shut up!" she cried. "What's the good of all that? Shut up, I tell you!"

"Has something happened?" Patrick asked, as he entered the gateway.

"We can't get into the store-room. I particularly told Christo that he must get those brats of Dino's out before today. Of course he did nothing about it. It really is too bad of him!"

"Poor Christo—he must have had enough to worry him, without thinking about that."

Dino had now gone to the small barred window, which was set high in the wall, and dragging himself up by his short yet massive arms, he started to shout: "If you don't come out of there at once, I'll give you such a hiding that you'll never forget it. Do you hear me, you ——?" He concluded with a curse, his normally roseate face purple from the combined effort of shouting and dangling from the bars. Then he dropped to the ground again, rubbing his hands against each other and dusting his clothes.

There was a silence, broken at last by a voice within shouting a single obscenity.

"I hadn't realized that there was someone inside," Patrick said. "I thought you meant that Christo had gone off with the key."

"It's that son of Dino's—Stavro. He's barricaded himself in. They want to break the door down, but that seems an unnecessary piece of destruction. After all, he'll have to come out sooner or later." Iris turned to Soula: "He hasn't any food in there, has he?"

There was a suppressed hysteria in Soula's voice as she replied: "He'd rather starve than give in. When he gets an idea—when he makes up his mind to something . . . And father shouldn't have shouted like that at him," she added in a whisper, so that Dino would not hear. "That was the worst thing to do. That was the worst thing of all."

"But why won't he come out?" Iris said. "I don't understand."

"It's been our room for so many years—not really our room, I know, it's your room—but . . . but I suppose . . ."

"Soula, there's no use your hanging about here, wasting the whole morning," her father broke off from a conversation with the builders to shout at her. "Get on down to the field. Your mother's already there. You've got an hour before the *Kyria* needs you in the surgery."

Soula gave a quick, bobbing curtsy and said to Iris again in a whisper: "It's best to leave him alone. The more you go at him, the worse he'll become. Leave him alone—I'll speak to him later!"

Iris walked over to the group of builders. It was extraordinary, Patrick thought, that such a trivial incident could produce this atmosphere of drama. Like practised swimmers in a rough sea, each of the onlookers seemed to take a pleasure in riding on crest after crest of useless emotion. Really one might have imagined that instead of a rebellious boy, a murderer was behind that locked door. "I have another job in the attic, you'd best get on with that." They stirred reluctantly, and made a thump and clatter with their ladders and paints; but then, as though at once forgetting what had been said to them, they resumed their discussion, each of their faces expressing a peculiar, solemn elation. "Come along!" Iris said.

Reluctantly, in ones and twos, they followed behind her. Patrick was alone with Dino who sighed and said:

"That boy's a great problem to me, sir. I wish you would advise me about him."

"What's wrong with him?" Patrick asked.

"What's wrong with him?" The man shook his head from side to side, pulled in his lips so that the unlit cheroot on which he was chewing was drawn for at least a third of its length into his mouth, and tilted his borsolino still further back on his head. "We've always done the best for him. We even sent him to the gymnasium in Corfu for two terms—that was as much as they would have of him. We're decent folk and we've tried to bring him up decent. But

not a week passes but he gets himself into some trouble or other."
He now took some matches from his pocket and lit the cheroot,
blowing out cloud after cloud of acrid smoke into Patrick's face,
as he went on: "He wants to go to sea. I was against it at first, but
now I think it may be the best thing for him. That's why I wanted
to have a word with you, sir. You know Mr. Typaldos, don't you?"

Patrick and Iris had met this shipowner in Athens and, when
they had left, he had insisted on giving them a *de luxe* cabin for
their journey to Corfu. But how had Dino come to hear of the
friendship?

"Yes. I know Typaldos," he said.

"I suppose you wouldn't be writing to put in a word for my
boy, sir, would you? It's hard to get work in the Merchant Navy,
but I'm sure that with your recommendation . . . It's not that he's a
bad lad," he continued, evidently sensing Patrick's hesitation. "He's
just wild. A few years at sea might be the making of him."

"I'll see what I can do."

Dino thanked him, taking one of his hands between both of
his own and pumping it up and down; then he went on to discuss
the orange-picking. He rattled off the names of labourers, sums
of money and dates, saying from time to time: "But that's up to
you, boss," to which Patrick replied: "No, I leave it to you. I know
nothing whatever about it." There was complete silence from the
store-room at the door of which they were talking.

"Well, I must be on my way. We've a big catch of 'kephalos'
lying ready in the lake. If madam would like some for supper, I'll
send some with the girl. There's no fish like 'kephalos', is there,
sir?"

After breakfast Patrick could settle to nothing. He read the
centre page of *The Times*, six days old; he went into his dark-room
but, having pottered around for a while, came out again; even
some new records of German *lieder* which had just arrived failed
to hold his attention. He no longer felt the depression of the night,
nor the sense of release of the morning, but rather a curious elation. Elation—but why? Then he remembered the faces of the
builders clustered outside the store-room.

He strolled out on to the verandah, righted a flower-pot which the wind had overturned, and taking the steps slowly, deliberately, with long pauses, he began to descend. From the open window of Iris's "surgery" he suddenly heard a horrible choking groan: it made his scalp tingle, his heart thump wildly.

He hesitated; then knocked on the store-room door. Silence. He put his ear to the door and still there was silence, except for the throb-throb-throb of the blood inside his head. "Stavro," he said. He spoke louder: "Stavro! Stavro, I want to speak to you!"

Once again silence. He pictured the boy, mutely obstinate, seated on a packing-case or crouched in a corner, with his large hands hanging between his knees and his hair tangled in a matted fringe across his forehead.

"Stavro—it's me. Mr. Orde. Let me in, will you?"

"What do you want? Go away. This room is mine."

"Well, let's have a chat about it."

"This room is mine," the boy repeated stubbornly.

"All right. But can't we have a five minutes' truce?"

"What's the point?"

"I've told you—I want to talk to you."

There was a long silence; then Patrick heard the sounds of heavy objects being moved away from the door, a key grated, a bolt was drawn away.

"Only five minutes," the boy said. "I trust you."

As he entered the vast, damp, badly-lit store-room, the smell that assailed Patrick's nostrils, though in no sense unpleasant, was like that of a place where animals habitate and he recollected how Christo had spoken of the room as the children's "den". Perhaps, he decided, that peculiar smell came from the bale of straw which lay mouldering in one corner; perhaps from the heap of seed-potatoes, green and sprouting maggot-like shoots. "So these are your head-quarters," he said. He looked around him, inquisitive and amazed.

There was a broken chair which he himself had had removed from his study, the leg now clumsily mended with two splints of wood lashed round with cord; another seat made of a packing-case covered with an old car-cushion, rusty springs pushing up through frayed leather; and a table, also made of a packing-case, supporting a white china teapot without a spout, an old Huntley and Palmer biscuit tin, a collection of clay pipes, many of them broken, a handle-less knife, a photographic spool and a catapult. The objects fixed to the walls were no less bizarre: a picture of Joe Louis taken from a cover of *Time* magazine; a calendar for the year 1937, depicting the British royal family on the faces of whom, male and female, moustaches and beards had been sketched in; the skin of a snake; a brochure, fastened neatly with four drawing-pins, of a patent-medicine ordered by Iris; and some snapshots, yellowed and curling at the edges, of a small boy hugging a goat, two monks, their eyes fixed protuberantly on the camera, Soula in peasant costume, and some sailors, their faces grey smudges as they leaned over the rail of a ship. On the wall above the fireplace the nude figure of a woman had been drawn in, life-size, with a gross and not unhumorous exaggeration of certain features.

Patrick spent the first minutes of the interview glancing surreptitiously at each of these pathetic objects in turn.

"May I sit down?"

"Please." The boy added: "But you speak good Greek."

"Do I? I didn't think it was good."

"You're English," the boy said. "How do you speak Greek?"

"Oh, I was often here before the war."

"As a spy?" The boy had the same green eyes as his sister: but while hers were usually lowered when she spoke to either Patrick or Iris, the boy's were challengingly direct.

Patrick laughed.

"Why do you laugh?"

"Because I'd make such a bad spy. . . . No, I was here collecting orchids."

"Orchids?"

"Yes, I'm a botanist." Patrick drew his cigarette-case out of his pocket, himself took a cigarette and then said to Stavro: "Would you like one?"

The boy hesitated, scowling at Patrick with his heavy brows as he obviously asked himself: what is the catch? Then he said: "Don't mind if I do."

"You usually smoke a pipe?" Patrick said, pointing to the collection on the packing-case before him.

"When I can get the tobacco."

"How old are you?"

"Nineteen."

Patrick knew this to be a lie: the boy was sixteen.

"And you?" Stavro asked.

"Thirty-nine."

"My father is thirty-nine. But you look much younger than him."

"Do I?"

"And *Kyria* Iris?"

"She's thirty-six."

The boy whistled: in Corfu the peasant-women age quickly. "She doesn't look it," he said in obvious admiration. "She's beautiful," he added.

"You know why my wife wants this room, don't you?" Patrick said.

"Yes. But she's already got a room."

"It's really not big enough."

"There are other rooms in the house."

"The advantage of this room is that it's *not* in the house." Patrick continued to speak gently, continued to smile, although the boy had now begun to glare at him with what he could only suppose to be hatred. He spoke of Iris's work and how it was done to help the peasants; of Soula's share in it; and of the occasion when Stavro himself had come to the surgery to have a cut dressed. "I know it's asking a lot of you," he said in conclusion, "but if you could possibly help us—well, it won't be only us, but the whole village that will thank you."

"I've had this room for nine years," the boy said in sullen opposition: he put out a large raw hand, chapped and seamed from work, and with a blunt forefinger rolled the broken stem of the clay pipe back and forth on the packing-case table.

"I know. As I say, it's asking a lot of you. We're terribly sorry about it. The only compensation we can make"—he leant forward, his hands clasped together, sensing some sudden relaxation in the boy's attitude—"is to offer you another room. Not such a large room, I'm afraid, nor even such a nice one."

"But there's no other room."

"I was thinking of one of the attics."

"But that would be in the house."

"Does that matter? Do you mind that? I don't suppose we should disturb you—or you disturb us."

"I thought . . ." The boy got up and went to the window; standing on tip-toe, he looked out at the bare tops of the trees. Once again Patrick felt that curious elation, a flutter behind the eyes, a flutter in the wrists. He picked up the broken pipe-stem which the boy's finger had moved, and stared down at it. Stavro whistled a bar of a Greek popular dance, his hands in his pockets: he whistled, as he sang, slightly off the note, so that the jaunty tune was clouded and clogged with melancholy. At last he turned: "The trouble is my father."

"Your father? Why?"

"You heard what he said he'd do to me."

"He was angry. I don't suppose he really meant it."

The boy smiled, rocking back and forth on the heels of his massive, mud-caked boots, his hands still in his pockets. "Oh, he meant it all right. You don't know him."

"Still—you'll have to come out *some* time. So you might as well get it over."

"That door's strong—look, it's got four bolts. I put them there. And it's got this iron bar. I saw to that when the Germans were here. He'd have to pull the wall down to get at me."

"But you'd have to eat."

"Oh, I should manage. I've lots of things here. There's a well under the floor."

"Is there?"

"Of course I could escape, if the worst came to the worst. I could stow away in a liberty ship. I could even cross to Albania. It's only seven miles away. I could steal a motor-boat at Cassiope and cross to Albania. That would be easy." His face lost its moody secretiveness and began to glow with elation as, one by one, he went in pursuit of these fantasies. "There are a lot of things I could do. I don't want to be stuck in this hole for the rest of my life."

"Your father told me you wanted to be a sailor. I said that I'd speak to Typaldos about you. But, of course, if you . . ." Again Patrick leant forward, his hands clasped together: "Look—why don't you have a look at the attics, see what you feel about them?"

"But I've told you—you heard what my father said. He means it too."

"Oh, I'll square him. I promise you won't be punished. Don't you trust me?"

They looked at each other for several seconds, before the boy said: "Yes."

"Well, then . . ." Patrick gave a long sigh which expressed partly relief and partly the strange state of contentment into which he had all at once slipped. He got up, and put a hand on Stavro's shoulder: "I knew we could come to an agreement."

Stavro said: "But I must see the attics first."

"Of course." Patrick peered at one of the snapshots—that of the sailors leaning over the ship—and asked: "Did you take that yourself?"

"No. It was given to me by a friend. That's him." A stubby forefinger rested on the grey smudge of a face. "He was a Dane. We were good friends. He also gave me this." He produced from his belt a sheath-knife, the same which Patrick had seen him hurl repeatedly at a tree that first evening in the village. "Feel it—it's sharp." Patrick felt the razor-like edge. "I sharpened it myself. . . . My friend had a Leica," he said, as he replaced the knife in its sheath of plaited leather, with a cat-like twist of his body.

"Yes, I have a Leica too."

"Have you?" The boy was excited. "I bought a camera myself in Ipsos, from a French student—he was here last year with the Club Méditerranée. But it's no good. I'll show it to you—perhaps you can tell me what's wrong with it." He went to a corner of the room, and squatting began to prise up a floor-board. "That's it," he said. One of his knees had appeared through a jagged hole in his mud-stained, grease-stained khaki trousers.

"It has no lens," Patrick said. "Of course it can't take photographs." He examined the ancient Lodak. "And there's a crack in the bellows."

"Then it's no use?"

"No use."

"Could I get it mended?"

"It wouldn't be worthwhile. If you're interested in photography you can borrow my camera."

The boy seemed to ponder for a moment, still squatting beside the raised floor-board, with his head on one side before he said: "You don't mean that."

"Why shouldn't I mean it? Of course I mean it."

He got up, raising his hands to the flaps of his shirt-pockets and fiddling with the buttons as he said: "Aren't you afraid I might steal it?"

"No. Why?"

"I do steal things, you know." There seemed to be a peculiar subdued ferocity both in the way he spoke the words and in the gaze he had now fixed on Patrick. "They've told you that, haven't they?"

"No."

He laughed derisively: "I don't believe you."

Patrick made for the door. "I'll go and speak to your father. I'm going to develop and print some photographs this evening. Would it amuse you to help?" The boy said nothing: he had again taken his jack-knife out of its sheath and was now rattling it up and down the iron bars of the window with an ugly, grating noise, whistling as he did so. "Well?" Patrick said.

The boy turned. "Of course it would amuse me." He started to shave flakes of skin off a callous on his hand. He blew on his palm as he said: "What time shall I come?"

"Oh, about eight o'clock." On an impulse, Patrick added: "Bring your sister if you like."

At once the boy stopped scraping at his palm; he looked up, wary as an animal which as it approaches a trap suddenly picks up a human smell. Patrick had the sense that in a second he would plunge away, and quickly he added: "But perhaps that sort of thing doesn't interest her. Come alone, if you prefer."

"I shall see."

"Good. . . . And now I must go and have a word with your father."

Stavro drew back the four bolts, each appearing to have its own special grate and clank, and held the door open. "Good-bye," he said.

"Good-bye, Stavro . . . I'm glad this is all settled."

5

"REALLY, one would think I intended to sell the stuff on the black market!" Iris exclaimed. "That's five weeks it's been stuck in the Customs. What did Amanassiades say to you when you went down to see him?"

Patrick, who had been at the window of the drawing-room, gazing into the courtyard, a cigar between his fingers, turned round and said: "I told you. He promised to have the whole consignment released at once."

"Oh, those promises!" Iris sat at a heavy Victorian knee-hole desk, the lamp beside her gleaming on one cheek-bone, on the white round of a shoulder, on an elbow and the wire of the tray in which were stacked the letters she was answering.

"I'm so tired of them. Well"—she drew a piece of writing-paper towards her, hunched herself over it, and dipped her pen in ink—"now I suppose I must send him a stinker which will bring more promises. Then I shall write to Athens. Promises again. And by next summer perhaps I shall get the stuff—when it'll all be too old, and will have to be thrown away."

It was twenty-past eight and neither Stavro nor his sister had come. As Patrick looked down, the courtyard seemed like a tank slowly filling up with darkness, until a similar tide rose within himself, the black liquid pushing up, soundlessly and invisibly, from some source the existence of which he had never before suspected. He glanced across at Iris, intent on her letter; and he thought how plain she looked tonight, with a smudge of ink on one corner of her chin, her hair all untidy, and that voraciously intent expression which her face seemed to assume whenever she was engaged on what she always called "the job". "You're tired out," he said. "Why don't you let up?" He opened one half of the french windows and let the late autumn air, moist yet without a chill, rise up at him from the courtyard. "You'll pay for it in the end."

She continued to scratch at the sheet of writing-paper: one would expect her handwriting to be neat and firm, not wavering into these enormous elliptical loops which often encircled letters above or below them. Then she glanced across at him: "One pays for everything in the end," she said.

He went out through the french windows, blowing a puff of cigar-smoke before him, and descended, step by step, into the "tank" which had once been a courtyard. As the wind blew up in small gusts, the darkness seemed to sway from side to side, splashing against the walls to clot there like blood.

What had become of Stavro? The dark-room was prepared: but without the boy and (once again the purple-black liquid slapped from side to side, again the scab-like shadows clotted on the wall) without his sister, he had no wish to begin the whole tedious business of developing and printing. Really he had no wish to do anything: to read, to listen to music, to help Iris with her letters.

A bird—or was it a bat?—swooped across the courtyard: he kept seeing it, like one of those retinal spots which appear before one's eyes as one looks into sunshine. Hither and thither it darted, now losing itself in the darkness at the bottom of the courtyard and now scissoring into the pearl-grey air above, until it plunged out under the roadway just as Patrick himself emerged. There was a wonderful smell here, autumnal and melancholy, of a bonfire, and through the gloom he could see where in a patch of a field the last sticks writhed upon each other like incandescent worms as the wind blew through them. He walked slowly on, and the direction he took, so unconsciously, was towards the house where Stavro and Soula lived. Here was the scrap of land, sloping down to the road, where he had first seen Soula working, and there, near a tumbled-down shed, was the tree out of which Stavro's voice had floated, derisive and insinuating: *Après la guerre finie, soldat anglais parti* . . . He could hear it now, while he still watched that rag-like form, bird or bat, fluttering before him.

Suddenly a shadow detached itself from the shadow of the tree: an arm was raised—was it beckoning or waving? He heard a loud crack which (how strung-up he must be) made him jump as though it were a revolver-shot. Another crack followed, ending with a grunt.

There were three people there, he could see it all now: the girl cowering under the tree, the boy tied by the wrists to a post near the shed, and the man with the thong raised above him. It was a scene of an extraordinary horror yet beauty, the bare glimmering torso of the boy submissive to his father's savage onslaught: while the girl looked on and all around them the autumnal landscape, vague and soft in the late evening light, exhaled its odours of wood-smoke and dead leaves and apples rotting deep in grass. A timeless interval seemed to elapse as Patrick took in each of the details—the shirt hanging from the waist, the metal strap of the watch on Dino's uplifted wrist, and that hand of Soula's, still raised either to warn him to keep away or to beg him to intercede—and then again the thong cracked downwards. That horrible animal grunt; it seemed to make the whole landscape tingle, shiver, dissolve.

"Come closer!" It was Stavro speaking to him, in a voice that seemed to Patrick's horrified imagination to be breaking through bubble after bubble of blood. Again the whip descended. "I trusted you, you ——" An obscenity ended the sentence.

"Dino!" Patrick shouted. "Dino!" he shouted again.

The man looked round, seemingly dazed as though the blows had fallen not on his son's but his own back and shoulders; then he stumbled over the roots of the tree towards Patrick.

"What are you doing? You gave me your promise."

The man ran the thong of the whip through his clenched fist: he still seemed dazed, almost as if he did not recognize Patrick or understood what was said to him. Incoherently he muttered a phrase, something about "only what he deserves".

Then in a sudden fury Patrick found himself shouting at the man. Afterwards he could remember little of what he said, except that he had accused him of cruelty and bad faith, and told him that he did not deserve to have children. Strangely, Dino made no answer to these accusations, as he might so easily have done, telling Patrick to mind his own business. Instead he merely stood, head bowed and the whip held between both hands, as if it were now he who was taking a turn at receiving punishment. Patrick noticed that his whole vast body was convulsed from time to time by violently prolonged shudders, and that large beads of sweat were glistening on his eyebrows, his upper lip and the muscular tattooed forearms from which he had pushed back the sleeves of his khaki jersey.

When Patrick's rage had at last spent itself, he looked for the two children and saw that they had gone. Presumably Soula had released her brother. As Patrick still stared at the post to which the boy had been fastened (normally it was used for the tethering of donkeys) he felt Dino suddenly clasp his right hand between both of his.

"I'm sorry, boss." All at once apologies and excuses were cascading from him. "I know I shouldn't have done it, after that promise that I made you. But it's the only thing he understands. The whip's the only thing he understands." He kicked out at the leather thong which was now curled, like a broken spring, at his feet. "I don't know what to do with him, I'm sure. I try to be a good father. I hate having to beat him, I'm not a cruel man, honest I'm not . . ." His Greek had acquired a slightly nasal inflection from the years he had spent in the States, and now this was exaggerated as though by the struggle to suppress tears. There was something peculiarly repellent about the cringing self-abasement of this massive, red-faced peasant, his voice whining on and on and his usually bright and shrewd black eyes clouded and distraught.

Eventually Patrick succeeded in disengaging himself; and as he walked away the feelings of indignation and disgust and (yes, he must be honest) excitement that the scene had provoked in him, were curbed and at last gently coaxed into no more than a quiz-zical amusement. It was an unconscious process, of course, this persistent muting of any vivid emotional colour, and it was with no awareness of self-deception that he would tell himself that really how preposterous it had all been; after all, no doubt Dino was right, a flogging was the only thing that could teach a boy like that a lesson. Probably he shouldn't have interfered, it was no use trying to impose one's own arbitrary will on the private lives of people who, even if they were in one's employ, were also indis-pensable to one.

In the courtyard he was surprised, and also a little annoyed, since he had now decided that he had enough of this business, to find Soula crouched on the bottom of the steps obviously in wait for him. She got up as he walked through the archway and came towards him with that extraordinary sideways walk, as though she half-feared that a sudden hand would be raised to strike her. "He asked me to come," she mumbled. "He wanted me to say thank you to you. What he shouted out at you, he didn't mean."

"Oh, that's all right." Impelled by an inexplicable curiosity he asked: "And does—does your father do that sort of thing to you also?"

She would not look up at him. "Sometimes. Not often. More often to Stavro. But we're used to it. It doesn't matter. . . . Anyway, thank you—from us both." Before she ran off she gave an odd little bob of the head and something that was almost a curtsy.

He could hear her bare feet pattering over the cobbles long after his eyes could no longer see her. Mounting the stairs, he all at once felt tired, cold, peevish.

Iris was still at work: "I hadn't realized you'd gone out. I must have been talking to no one. I was reading you this letter and all the time you weren't there at all!"

Patrick fastened the catch of the window. "I went out for a stroll."

"Anywhere in particular?"

"No, nowhere in particular. Just for a stroll."

2

WINTER

I

OFTEN, afterwards, Patrick was astonished that it had been so easy to win the devotion of those two children. He had, after all, made no effort to do so; and he had never, in the past, had much faith in his ability to charm. He was a man in whom people seemed to sense a refusal ever to be fully committed, and though he rarely inspired dislike, he inspired affection even more rarely. Yet because of a few kind words, spoken (as he repeatedly told himself) entirely out of a sense of self-interest, the loan of a camera, and an intervention which he could hardly have avoided, he had bound two strangers to him far more closely than any friends he had ever had in his life. It was extraordinary: and there were times when he was frightened by a love so unsought, so unexpected, so unmanageable in all its odd implications.

His first realization of the strength of the tie had come in January, at the beginning of the rainy season. Patrick had been into the town on a shopping expedition, and when he had returned, driving the Rolls himself, since Christo was still in hospital, Stavro had run out from under the tunnel-like arch which led into the courtyard to help him unload. Since he had no waterproof, the boy had covered his head with a sack from which flour had dusted downwards to coat his thick eyebrows and eyelashes and the bridge of his nose.

"Don't bother, Stavro. You'll get awfully wet. I can do it alone."

"I'm not made of sugar."

"Well, take my old mackintosh then. It's hanging in the hall."

Stavro laughed as he tugged a box of groceries out of the back of the car. "We're used to rain in Corfu."

"Oh, damn!" Patrick said, as they sorted the things indoors. "I knew I'd forgotten something. The developer is here, but I never asked for that bromide paper. And I'd particularly wanted to do those enlargements this evening. I suppose nobody's driving into the town this afternoon?"

"I can ask for you at the café."

"Would you? That would be most awfully kind."

After dinner that evening, Anna, the maid, announced to Patrick that Stavro wished to see him. Patrick went down to the hall and found the boy standing in a pool of water, his clothes stuck to his body and his hair stuck to his forehead in four ragged prongs. He smiled showing his magnificently white, even teeth and held out a package that was wrapped round and round in a sack. "I got it for you," he said.

"What is it?"

"The bromide paper."

"Do you mean you——? Did someone give you a lift?"

"No, I bicycled in."

"But the road must have been impassable. I could barely drive up it. And it's eleven miles, mostly up and down hill!"

Patrick was appalled.

"Oh, that's nothing. Don't worry about that." He continued to say it was nothing, whenever Patrick tried to thank him, shaking his body from time to time like a dog and running his hands through his dripping hair.

"Come into the kitchen and change those clothes. I'll give you some of mine. You'd better drink something."

"Some whisky?"

"If you like," Patrick laughed.

"My Danish friend once gave me some whisky. I don't really like the taste. It smells of squashed bugs."

"I don't think I've ever smelled a squashed bug."

"You'd have smelled one all right, if you'd lived in our house."

When Patrick returned to the drawing-room, he told Iris of Stavro's ride to the town, concluding: "What wonderful people they are!"

"Stavro and Soula?"

"No, not only Stavro and Soula. The Greeks as a race. I find

I admire them more and more. They have so much dignity and courage—and such a capacity for joy."

"You'd probably take a less rosy view of them if you had to answer all these letters." She pointed to the heap before her. "Anyway, I agree that we couldn't manage without Stavro and Soula. She's become an awfully good little nurse. You know, I'm glad that hunch of mine turned out so well." She sighed: "I only wish Dino were equally reliable."

Through the weeks since Christo had left for hospital Iris had increasingly had cause to complain of Dino's work as bailiff. It was, she and Patrick had at first told each other, unreasonable to expect from him a devotion comparable to Christo's: Christo was an exception, he had lived only for them and the work of the estate, whereas Dino had his family, his own property, interests of his own. Dino's careless, they would say, he's happy-go-lucky, improvident: but what Greek is not? Yet their dissatisfaction with him grew. Although neither of them gave the accounts more than a cursory look-over, and although, when Dino came to them to talk about the hiring of labour, the sale of their oranges or the buying of fertilizer, they usually agreed with everything he suggested, yet it became impossible to ignore the fact that the estate was doing badly. Week by week, profits seemed to dwindle until soon the time came when money was actually being lost. Dino was glib with his explanations: this was the wrong season, the Merlin estates had flooded the market with oranges and no one now would buy, the olive-crop had been poor. When they questioned him more closely, his jolly red face would become even redder and he would push back his borsolino as he asked, with a mixture of truculence and injured loyalty: Perhaps they didn't trust him? No, of course they trusted him, they would both at once say. Hadn't his family served Iris's for centuries? he would next demand. Of course, of course, they would say. It wasn't that. They never for a moment questioned his honesty. They were worried, that was all.

"Do you think he's doing us down?" Iris now asked.

"Who can say? We know so little about the way the estate is run. You're too busy to go into the whole thing thoroughly, and

I've been too lazy. . . . Why don't you ask your mother? She seems to run her own place most efficiently."

"No." There was in the monosyllable an extraordinary hardness and coldness which Patrick had always sensed, but now for the first time saw revealed, in Iris's attitude to her mother. It was odd that one word should have brought that revelation, when so many others had failed to do so.

"Why on earth not?"

"Because I don't want mother interfering in our affairs. When she does interfere, it's rarely to the advantage of anyone but herself."

"Have you had a quarrel?"

"No. Why?"

Patrick mused for a while, rearranging the logs blazing in the open hearth; then he said: "Shall I ask Christo?"

"Ask him? Ask him what?"

"His opinion. I'll say that we're worried by this drop in our profits. I could take him the accounts."

"Don't forget that he's Dino's brother. Anyway, he's far too ill to be worried over that sort of thing. No, you'd better not mention the subject to him."

"He's still terribly interested in the estate. He's always asking me about it. . . . You know, Iris"—he went over to where she sat at her desk and put his hands on her shoulders—"I do think you might go in and see him."

She fidgeted under his touch and said: "Your fingers are cold." Her pen began to scratch over the paper.

But he pursued: "When I go in next Saturday, why don't you come with me? He keeps wanting to know how you are and what you are doing. He must think it odd that you've never once made the effort."

"But I'm busy—you know how busy I am!" She swung round in the chair, her usually placid face looking almost ugly as it was churned by the annoyance of her protest. "And he must know how busy I am. I've been into town only once in all the time that he's been laid up—and that was to see the Prefect about that building licence. If there were anything I could do to help him, I'd go—of course I'd go. But Petropoulos is an excellent doctor; he's in the best possible hands."

Patrick sighed: "Poor Christo! . . . Look, why don't you come with me next Saturday? It's Soula's name-day and I said that I'd take the two children into the cinema to see *Alice in Wonderland*. We can call in at the hospital before the performance."

"Oh, really, I've better things to do than see *Alice in Wonderland*. And I'm sure the two children would much prefer a Western," she added irrelevantly.

All at once Patrick felt furious with her—"I suppose you realize that Christo may be dying."

"Yes, I had realized that." She looked up at him with a smile that seemed to carry with it an extraordinary contempt: "After all, I think I know a little more about medicine than you do, don't I?"

2

STAVRO was wearing a blue serge suit that had once been his father's, shiny at the elbows, the collar and knees, a white flannel shirt, and a hand-painted silk tie which, he said, had been given him by his Danish sailor-friend. He produced the tie from his pocket as they were getting into the car, and asked Patrick to make the knot for him. "I can't manage the thing," he murmured in the sulky growl that Patrick now knew he used whenever he wished to conceal his embarrassment. "It's the first time I've worn it." The ends of his collar would not meet across his throat and having made a number of futile attempts to tug them together, Patrick left a gap. Standing close to the boy like this, he was once again aware of that peculiar animal-like smell that clung to the "den"—a smell, not unpleasurable, that was associated in his mind with the fur of animals in the south.

Soula had on a plain black frock, the skirt unfashionably short to reveal her knees and the bodice tight across breasts which, Patrick had noticed, had grown perceptibly even during these few weeks since he and Iris had arrived in Corfu. She had a white handkerchief fastened by four clips over her luxuriant tawny hair,

and she wore black woollen stockings that seemed hideous on legs
that he had grown accustomed to seeing smooth and brown and
bare. She was carrying a handbag of cheap, shiny leather already
criss-crossed with white lines where it had cracked in spite of its
obvious newness.

"You can get in behind," Stavro said to his sister. "I want to
watch how it works." He opened the front door for himself.

Patrick could see that Soula was disappointed and he put in:
"There's room for all three in front—if you don't mind a crush."

"Oh, she doesn't mind sitting in the back. She's not interested in
cars. In you go, Soula!"

Soula got in behind.

When they reached the hospital, Stavro was obviously reluctant to come in and see his uncle. "We'll only tire him," he said.
"Soula and I can wait here and watch the tennis, until you get
back." Opposite the hospital there was a hard-court on which four
squat, hairy men in white shorts, singlets and white peaked caps
were running tirelessly up and down. "Perhaps you could take
these things up for us—mother sent them." He handed Patrick a
basket.

"But don't you think your uncle would like to see you?"

The boy grinned: "I was never a favourite of his. . . . Anyway,
that hospital gives me the creeps." All at once he looked surly, as
he kicked at a tyre of the car with one of the blunt toes of his
heavy black boots.

It was not unusual, Patrick had discovered, for Greeks to have
this abhorrence not only of illness, but of those who were ill: and
he wondered now if Iris, in spite of her work for the sick, was
still sufficiently Greek to share in that feeling. Perhaps that would
explain the seeming callousness of her refusal to visit Christo.

"You'll come with me, won't you, Soula?"

"No, Soula can wait here with me."

The girl looked from her brother to the Englishman and then
back to her brother, wondering whom to obey. Patrick suffered a
sudden violent spasm of annoyance against the boy. "Let's allow
Soula to decide for herself," he said.

She hesitated; then: "I'll stay with Stavro," she murmured in an almost inaudible voice.

"As you wish."

When, having traversed the whole length of the ward, Patrick at last came up to Christo's bed, he wondered if his face expressed an involuntary disgust for, once they had greeted each other, the sick man's first words were: "I'm sorry to have to bring you to this horrible place."

"It's not so horrible. You seem very comfortably situated. And your Sister is charming—I've just been having a word with her." The phrases sounded glib and meaningless as Patrick began to unpack the basket and place the things on a shelf beside the bed. "You're looking so much better. You've got your colour back. And you've put on weight, haven't you?"

"No, I don't think so."

"Stavro and Soula are with me. They didn't come up because they thought that they would tire you. So they asked me to bring you their best wishes and their love. These things are from their mother."

"Thank you."

During the weeks he had been in hospital Christo's skin had turned a curious purplish-brown colour, and his mouth, his nostrils and his eye-sockets seemed to have enlarged out of all proportion to the rest of his face.

"Are you feeling better?" Patrick sat on the locker which each patient had at the bottom of his bed and in an attempt to appear at his ease, smiled first at Christo and then gazed about him. In the next bed an old man was propped, skinny and unshaven, with a rubber tube protruding from one nostril. Patrick looked away.

"No. I'm feeling worse."

"But surely—both Petropoulos and the Sister tell me that you've got over the operation quite remarkably well."

Christo gave a small twitch of the lips which might express either annoyance or amusement; then he closed his eyes: "It was a mistake for me to have had it. I knew it would be no use. I'd have preferred to die at home."

As Patrick looked at the emaciated, purplish-brown face, the closed eyelids almost black in hue against the surrounding skin, his first emotion was not one of sympathy or even pity for the other man in his despair, but merely of outrage. This was not playing the game; hospital patients, however ill, did not talk like this; it was as bad as taking off a bandage and forcing a visitor to look down into some horrible wound or ulcer. "What nonsense!" Patrick said. "You're not going to die. You mustn't talk like that. You mustn't give way, you know. There's always hope—and in your case, Petropoulos holds out every hope of an absolute recovery."

"I shall never recover. And you—and Petropoulos—know it as well as I do. I shall die here—like a poisoned rat in a hole." There was a terrible bleakness and cruelty and hopelessness in the words; and there was also, Patrick realized, a no less terrible strength. It was not cowardice, but courage, that enabled him to face death in despair, without a single self-deception for comfort.

Resting by his feet Patrick had the portfolio in which he had brought down the accounts he and Iris had decided to show to Christo; but now the whole question of the estate, dwindling profits and Dino's honesty seemed remote and trivial. At that moment it had become as impossible to communicate with Christo as if he had already passed into that annihilation which, it was obvious, was all that he now foresaw for himself.

"How is Iris?"

The sudden question astonished Patrick: it was the only time that he had ever heard Christo speak of her as anything other than "the *Kyria*" or "*Kyria* Iris".

"She's well. But terribly busy. She asked me to say how sorry she was that she hasn't been along to see you. You know she has this dispensary of hers, and she's at it from morning till night. Frankly I'm worried about her; I think she works too hard. She's only been into town once, all the time we've been here. I'm taking Soula and Stavro to *Alice in Wonderland* this evening—a name-day treat for Soula—and I tried to persuade my wife to come too." He had hesitated momentarily, unsure whether to say "my wife" or "Iris". "But I wouldn't get her to budge. She's far too conscientious."

"I should like to have seen her, just once."

"She'll come down next week—these last few days she's had

an awful rush of patients. There's an epidemic of measles among the children and that keeps her extra busy." As he talked Patrick fiddled uneasily with the catch of the locker on which he sat.

"She'll never come. I shall never see her again."

There was a long silence.

Then, all at once, Christo raised himself on one elbow and began to question Patrick about the village: his despair seemed to have passed, and his interest in all his old associations to have miraculously revived. He laughed, often with a dry, choking sound that was almost like a cough, and his eyes, which had been withdrawn and clouded by his terrible acceptance of death, now began to glitter brilliantly as Patrick recounted the story of a feud between the owner of the café and his next-door neighbour over a mule. He asked about a number of trivial details of the olive-harvest—had they employed old Spiro, what yield had they had from this or that tree?—and then he wanted to know if Patrick and Iris were satisfied with Dino. Patrick explained about the drop in profits and produced the accounts for the last few weeks.

"You must never trust Dino," Christo said, as he stared at the first account. "You know that, don't you?" It seemed a strange thing for a man to say of his brother. "Never trust him." He stared at the iron rail at the bottom of his bed, and slowly his eyes again clouded and took on that strangely secretive, withdrawn expression. He pushed the accounts away from him. "I can't look at them now." He lowered his head back on to his pillow and his tongue scraped the corners of his mouth as though for invisible crumbs. Eventually he said: "I think you'd better go."

"Good-bye, Christo. Is there anything you want—anything I can do for you?"

"Nothing—now."

There was something mysterious and almost accusing in the addition of that last single word.

"Good-bye, then. Get better. We want you back soon."

Christo's lips twitched: he seemed to have been about to grimace, and then to have restrained himself. "Good-bye."

Patrick blinked as he stepped back into the sunshine; he raised a hand to his eyes. The four squat, hairy men were resting beside the tennis-court, two seated on a bench and two lying in the grass, while Soula and Stavro knocked a ball back and forth across the net. It was obvious that this was a game which neither of them had ever played, and they laughed and shouted to each other as the ball shot off their rackets high into the air. Stavro had taken off his blue-serge coat and the knot of his hand-painted silk tie had descended to the second button of his shirt: Soula's luxuriant hair had fallen from under its handkerchief and she kept brushing it away from her cheeks and eyes with her left hand as she swung the racket in her right.

As Patrick stood outside the door of the hospital and watched, he thought how beautiful they looked, in their youth and animal grace and vigour. Tirelessly they ran after the ball, while the sun flashed on their bare arms, their teeth and their hair. Even in these few minutes they had taught themselves much of the game. All at once Soula saw him and she called out, with none of her usual shyness: "Come along and join us!"

Slowly at first, and then breaking into a trot, he crossed the road from the hospital to the tennis-court.

Standing in front of Patrick in the queue at the box-office of the cinema was one of the officer-cadets from the fortress. He was a tall, blond young man with a thick neck the back of which had a raw, rubbed look as though a pair of clippers had just been over it. While they waited he spent his time smoothing out a number of crumpled and grubby five-hundred and thousand drachmae notes between hands that were large and pink and fleshy.

When he had bought his ticket, he turned and saw Soula, nodded, smiled and said "Yassoo" to her.

Soula murmured "Yassoo": she glanced momentarily at him, and then looked down again as she began to fiddle with one of the slides that fastened the handkerchief over her hair.

"Who was that?" Stavro demanded.

"I don't know his name."

"Why did he greet you?"

"Oh, once he came to the house for some water. They were having some sort of exercise near the village."

"I don't remember."

"You weren't there. It was while you were still working at the docks."

"How does he remember you?"

"Why shouldn't he remember me?"

"Did you speak to him?"

"I drew the water for him from the well, and we may have chattered a little."

"Shall I sit between you?" Patrick said. He felt that if he did not separate them, they might soon begin to quarrel. "How about some ice-creams?" As he looked round to attract the attention of the boy-vendor, he noticed that the young officer-cadet had moved up into a seat directly behind Soula. He had taken a newspaper out of his pocket and was studying the football scores, his small blue eyes screwed up in his stupid yet not unattractive face and his small teeth biting on the corners of his blond moustache. As Patrick paid the vendor, he saw out of the corner of his eye that the officer had taken out a diary, and having torn out an old sheet, was scribbling on it in pencil.

At that moment the lights went out.

Patrick glanced in turn at the children on either side of him: and he was amazed to find that their reactions to the film were exactly the opposite of what he had expected. The boy was absorbed, sitting motionless, while the remains of his ice-cream melted in the tub he grasped in his hand; his lips were slightly parted, his eyes glittered with an extraordinary brilliance through the surrounding darkness. Soula, on the other hand, did nothing but fidget. For a long time Patrick could hear her rattling the wooden spoon in her ice-cream tub; then the tub was dropped, and she began to scratch her left forearm with her right hand; she shifted uneasily, sighed and crossed and recrossed her legs.

It was while she was thus shifting that her knee suddenly struck against Patrick's. At once he jerked his own knee away; but a moment later he was easing it gently back, while his heart thumped louder and louder and his eyes ached more and more from staring fixedly at the screen before him. He could feel, with an extraordinary hyperaesthesia, her dress brushing the cloth of his trousers; he could even feel a warmth given out by her flesh, so close now to him. Again he shifted his knee away; glanced at Stavro who was still absorbed in the picture, one hand fiddling with the collar-button of his shirt; and then eased the knee back. Now there was a real contact, not of cloth on cloth, but of flesh touching flesh. He pressed and there seemed to be an answering pressure. Once again he pressed. The rest of Soula's body was absolutely still; she seemed to be as absorbed as her brother in the film, but for that persistent exertion and withdrawal of pressure in response to his own.

He coughed and blew his nose, and used his handkerchief to wipe the sweat that was streaming down his forehead. He put a hand on his knee, and let it, inch by inch, topple over until the little finger was resting on her body. She did not move away; and a second later she shifted further down in her seat so that his hand was resting far up her thigh. It was a madness, but he could not restrain himself; he began to move his hand.

When the lights came up for the interval during which the reels were changed, Patrick was trembling and his face seemed to be on fire. He was terrified of even looking at Soula. But with an extraordinary composure, she leant across him to ask her brother: "Are you enjoying it?"

"Very much. And you?"

She swayed her head gently from side to side and drew down the corners of her mouth as Greeks do when they are uncertain of an opinion. "And you, *Kyrie* Orde? Do you like the film?"

Patrick said: "Oh, yes, yes, yes." If he had been asked to describe a single scene from the work, he would have been unable to do so. His eyes had been conscious of a changing brightness, his ears of a noise that had seemed to expand and retract like something within his own head: that was all. "Shall we go out for some air?"

They walked up and down the road outside the cinema, and Patrick was conscious, as Stavro obviously was not, that all the time the young officer-cadet was walking behind them. He had put on his cap, low over his forehead, and as he walked he swung the chain of a bunch of keys in his right hand and whistled a Greek popular song. Stavro was questioning Patrick about the process of making a full-length cartoon film, but a combination of ignorance and agitation made the Englishman's replies wholly unintelligible. Stavro's forehead was puckered as his confusion grew. From time to time he would say: "I know I'm being awfully stupid, but I just don't understand . . ."

Soula, who seemed to be as unaware as Stavro that her officer-cadet was following, began to tease her brother with a boldness that she had never before shown in Patrick's presence. "Well, I'm glad to hear you admit for once that you're stupid. Haven't I always told you so? . . . You know, *Kyrie* Orde, he never got beyond his first year at the gymnasium. After that, they asked him to leave."

"That wasn't for stupidity!"

"Only a donkey would make love to that awful Zaira Kraktopoulou."

"Who said I made love to her?"

"She did! Anyway, do you deny that you always used to see her home? Do you?"

"Well, if you'd been the daughter of the richest grocer in Corfu, perhaps some boy might have been persuaded to see even *you* home from school."

Their heavy banter began to take on a faintly improper tinge as they shouted at each other across Patrick and burst into peals of laughter. He had often enough seen Stavro in this mood, for the boy had long since overcome any feelings of restraint in the Englishman's presence; but it was the first time that Soula's nature had been revealed to him unmuted by obsequiousness and shyness.

As the lights went out again, Patrick was addressing Stavro; but he had the sensation—he was never to be certain—that in that moment when his head was turned sideways, the officer-cadet had leant forward and either whispered something to Soula or handed something to her. Patrick remembered how he had seen the man scribble on a sheet torn from his diary, and the suspicion came to him that perhaps he had passed Soula a note. But now, as he looked at her searchingly, her face seemed impassive in the reflected flicker of the screen; her hands lay crossed quietly in her lap; her body was relaxed. It could not be so. Yet had she not shown a similar tranquillity at his caresses?

Thinking now of that dangerous, thrilling contact of his flesh on hers, he put off his suspicions as a bather puts off his clothes before plunging into the sea. Perhaps there was some secret between Soula and the cadet, perhaps there was not. What did it matter? Why should he care? What was it to him at this moment, when by moving his arm six inches, shifting his body to an almost imperceptible angle right-wards, he could renew a pleasure so violent as to be almost a kind of physical agony? Years afterwards he would remember those minutes in the darkened cinema: the constriction of clothes, the sudden warmth of flesh; her parted lips and the rise and fall of her breast and her quickened breathing as she continued to stare at the screen while his hand moved over her; her own fingers, tentative at first and then insistent; the geography of the palm of one of her hands, with the callouses at the base of the middle- and the wedding-finger, the closely-cut nails and the roughness that contrasted so wonderfully with the smoothness of wrist and forearm. He felt sick, vaguely dizzy, and yet overflowing with a heedless euphoria, as one does when one comes round from an anaesthetic; and deep within himself he could feel, sleeping, the agony which, also as after an anaesthetic, would thaw out, slowly, slowly, and then leap to a terrible, destroying life.

It was dark when they left the cinema. "I must go to the Club," Patrick said, "to pick up an overcoat I left there. You both go and drink a lemonade and eat a cake at 'Caprice' and I'll come back and join you. All right?"

"Can't I go to the Club for your coat?" Stavro suggested.

"No, it's very kind of you, but they might not let you in. I'm not even sure where I left it. It won't take me a moment in the car."

Before driving off, he sat at the wheel and gazed after them as they walked, hand unselfconsciously linked to hand by the little fingers, down the arcade to a table outside the café he had named. They looked embarrassed as they sat down to the table, Stavro perpetually brushing his hair off his forehead with one of his large hands while Soula tugged at the hem of her skirt: Patrick guessed that this was the first time they had ever sat at one of these cafés that looked out over the main square, for the peasants never used them, preferring the square called San Roco, with its overloaded and ramshackle buses drawn up on a baked rectangle of mud, its stalls where vegetables and fruit and gaudy lengths of cotton were sold, and its men and women chattering in groups around their horse-drawn carts. As he drove off, he marvelled that Soula's only unease should be caused by a strange environment, while he himself churned in this state of ever-increasing turmoil, like a bather now flung from crest to crest of the waves and now dashed downwards into a green and icy abyss of terror, while the shore receded further and further from him.

His coat was in the library of the Club, and as he picked it up, the Harbourmaster, who was reading an old copy of *Punch*, got to his feet and called: "Hello, there! Why do we never see you? The young men are all playing ping-pong, and the old women are all playing bridge. I feel so bored." He put a comradely arm around Patrick's shoulder: "Come upstairs, let me buy you a drink. They've got some whisky in."

Patrick was about to answer when the door opened and Doctor Petropoulos appeared, some books under his arm. He was timid in company and now seemed to be hesitating whether to greet them or ignore them. But the Harbourmaster said: "And here's our friend the doctor! He's like you—he never comes here. Except for his books."

"Good evening, Doctor."

"Good evening." Petropoulos put his books down on a table and began to tick them off in the registry, murmuring as he did so: "I'm afraid that poor chap's gone."

"What chap?"

"That man from your village."

"Gone?" Obtusely, Patrick still could not understand.

"Yes. Less than an hour ago." He ran a finger down the registry: "Can't find this book—oh, here it is! . . . Yes, a coronary thrombosis. Just as well, really. He'd have died in terrible agony. It so often happens after that operation, a clot of that kind." He looked up and at once realized that to Patrick Christo must have been something more than just someone from his village; and being a kind and humane man, he at once hastened to make some amends for the objectivity with which he had described Christo's end. "I'm sorry," he said. "It was all so pointless, too—it *needn't* have ended like that. If only he'd come to me three months earlier, when he first had the pain. But they're so frightened these peasants, they always come too late."

The Harbourmaster said: "Come—let's go for that drink."

"No, really, I must get back to the hospital."

"And I have some friends who are waiting for me," Patrick said.

Patrick walked with Petropoulos towards the main square. At first they did not speak, the Englishman because of shock and the Greek because of shyness; but as they were about to part, the Greek said: "Yes, I'm sorry. There are times when I wonder why I took up this profession. You're wise to live as you live—with your music and your botany and your photography. I wish I had had the sense to do the same." He took Patrick's hand: "Now I must leave you. You'll tell the family, I suppose. Will you?"

"Yes, I'll tell the family."

It was only now that Patrick realized that two members of the family were waiting for him at the café.

He went across slowly and sat down between them. They had finished their cakes, but before their smeared plates there were two glasses, misty with iced water, and Patrick took one of these, Soula's, and sipped from it. "The cakes were wonderful," Stavro said. "I'm afraid we've eaten three each."

Patrick smiled faintly. Then, having sipped again at the water, he said: "I've just seen Doctor Petropoulos."

"Yes, we saw you with him."

Patrick hesitated: "He gave me some bad news. . . . Your uncle is dead."

Ever since the scene with the gipsy-girl, Patrick had grown accustomed to the violent paroxysms of grief into which these peasants retreated when faced with death or separation—had he not seen a woman roll over and over on the earth with terrible lamentations when her son left to do his military service?—and he had expected the two children to exhibit the same lack of restraint. But they merely gazed at him with a kind of stunned bewilderment. Perhaps, Patrick thought, the shock had been too great for them; perhaps, after all, they had never cared for Christo.

Stavro said at last: "I think we ought to go—if you don't mind. We have some jobs to do with the animals before turning in for the night. . . . We shall pay for our cakes," he restrained Patrick as the Englishman took out his wallet.

Patrick nonetheless insisted on paying.

They drove back almost without speaking. Once Stavro pointed and said: "A man killed his wife in that house, only last year," but Patrick merely answered: "Oh, yes" and did not ask for the story. Another time Stavro said: "You English believe in ghosts, don't you?" and Patrick murmured: "Some of us" to which Stavro replied: "No Greeks do." The Englishman felt a disgust so violent that it was almost a kind of physical nausea: but whether this disgust was for his own behaviour in the cinema, for the circumstances of Christo's illness and death, or for the apparent callousness of these children, sitting so tranquil beside him, he could not yet decide.

"Thank you, *Kyrie* Orde. We've enjoyed it so much." Momentarily he was holding that hand every contour of which he had explored in the darkened cinema; then he was holding Stavro's. Anna had come out at the sound of the car, and was standing on the terrace above the courtyard; Patrick called out to her: "Is the *Kyria* in the house?" It was Iris, not he, who would have to break the news of Christo's death to the family: from the first he had assumed that.

"She's gone out for a walk."

"For a walk! At this hour! It's nearly ten o'clock." He was astonished.

"She took the path down to the lake."

"I'll see if I can find her."

It was only when he was halfway down the hillside that he realized that there was no need to go in search of Iris; already the children would have told their parents the news, already the village would have heard. But still he walked on, stumbling in the darkness over the stones that strewed the pathway and clutching from time to time at a bush or an overhanging branch.

There was no moon yet, but a subdued light came off the lake as though it were part of the same exhalation that had scarfed its furthest edges with mist. Patrick's feet rang out on the causeway, causing a clatter of wings and a rustle of spray from some rushes which stuck up, like iron spikes, out of the shallows beneath. The sea on the right was almost as placid as the lake on the left and for a stranger, in that light, it would have been difficult to decide which was which. The two smells, tang of salt and bitterness of decay, seemed inseparable, mingling with each other as the water mingled with the sky, the earth with the water, the sky with the earth, each lost in the other and creating this mist that seemed to partake of each.

"Iris! Iris!" He put his hands to his mouth, and shouted louder and louder, and again there was that clatter of wings and turbulence of water, until two white shapes, wild geese, lumbered out of the reeds and flapped out into the luminous desolation of the lake where they alighted in ever-widening concentric circles.

Someone was walking towards him down the causeway, and he began to hasten on. "Iris!"

"Yes. . . . You've spoiled it all with your shouting." Now, all at once, she was near him, her broad forehead and her arms gleaming like the geese beyond her. "It was so wonderful a moment ago."

"I'm sorry. Anna told me you had come down here for a stroll, and I thought that I'd join you. The last time we were here together was the first evening we arrived—remember?"

"Yes, I remember."

"Then it was like the last day of autumn. And now it feels like the first day of spring. . . . It's not at all cold, is it?"

"Not at all." But as he slipped his arm through hers, she gave an involuntary shudder. "Good film?" she asked.

"Oh, yes, yes," he said vaguely. "I think the children enjoyed it. . . . Iris—what I came to tell you was—Christo is dead."

She said nothing, but merely walked on, back along the causeway, freeing her arm from his and drawing the ends of the stole she was wearing closer about her.

Behind, Patrick explained: "I met Petropoulos at the Club, it was he who told me. Coronary thrombosis. I suppose it was really just as well, going like that . . ." He talked on, conscious of something amiss yet not knowing what; afraid of the silence of the mingling lake and sky, of the two geese motionless, of the woman before him. Louder and louder his voice rang out, saying all the conventional things with which people attempt to fill the silence of death, and the hills around sent his voice back to him with a sound like a muffled drum.

They had come to the place where four stepping-stones traversed a brook which ran into the lake with a monotonous drip and gurgle, and his shoes sinking into mud, he put out an arm to assist Iris over. But she snatched her hand from him:

"Leave me!" she cried with a kind of childish fretfulness. "I can manage alone!"

For a moment her face was no longer set in its usual calm, resolute lines; and in that moment understanding came to him, the sleeping agony awoke.

Soon after eleven that evening an icy wind from the Albanian mountains swept through the village. Shutters banged, branches creaked, a tile swept off the roof and crashed into the courtyard. Patrick got up and went to shut the windows of the bedroom. Almond blossom whirled through the dark before him, mingling with dust and dead leaves. He could hear the hood of the car flapping; the dog rattling its chain in its kennel under the archway; and, so he imagined, the distant roar and thud of the waves. He listened, shivering now in his pyjamas, with a hand on the latch of the window. Merging into these sounds, he thought he could hear singing. He wandered out on to the balcony. Then, of course, he realized. In Dino's house, the lights were still burning: and the sounds of lamentation were borne out into the night on gust after gust of ice-laden wind. Through the long, dark hours they would pour out their grief in a single bitter flood; and in the morning they would go out, weak and dizzy with exhaustion, but exalted and purified and strengthened.

He went back and stretched himself on the bed alongside Iris. There were no tears on her cheeks, and though he knew she was not sleeping, she made neither sound nor move.

3

"Yes, it certainly looks as if the rascal had been cheating you. You must have got more than two million for your oranges—that's barely fifty pounds. I got eleven million. And I've only half your number of trees." Mrs. Nicolidou put the last spray of almond-blossom into the copper jug and, wiping her large hands, encrusted with their rings, down her apron, said: "That's pretty, isn't it?"

"Very pretty."

"I told you Dino was not to be trusted, didn't I? But Iris always thinks she knows best. I no longer try to give her advice—I know she'll never take it. . . . And that bill for paraffin, there's something wrong there," she went on. "You can't have used all that. He's done a fiddle with old Vlachos." It was strange to hear the old lady use this last colloquialism, no doubt the fruit of her enthusiastic reading of English detective novels. "It's a pity you decided against running the estate yourself—that was the original idea, wasn't it?"

"Yes, but then Christo seemed to be doing it so well. . . ."

"Ah, Christo!" She made an eloquent gesture, raising both her hands and then letting them fall to her sides. "He was a bailiff in a thousand."

"What do you think should be done about Dino?"

"You must talk to him," she replied decisively. "Let's go out. I must see the stable-boy. . . . Yes, you must talk to him. No use beating about the bush in Greece. Plain speaking, that's what the Greeks like. Dino will probably be furious to begin with, but in a day or two. . . . Talk to him, that's what you must do, talk to him."

"I don't quite see how I can put it!"

"Be jocular, that's the best way. Go up to him and say: 'Look here, you old rascal, you've been cheating us all these weeks. Now don't try to deny it. And it's time that you stopped.' Don't be too serious or stern—say it in the friendliest possible way. Jocularity, that's the thing, jocularity."

Patrick had never found it easy to be jocular, and he knew that it would be impossible for him to be so while accusing another man of dishonesty. Unconsciously he decided that this task, too, would have to be left to Iris.

They passed a shed, dark and evil-smelling, inside which animals could be heard moving uneasily; but it was impossible to see what animals they were. Mrs. Nicolidou was picking her way carefully over stones, heaps of manure and puddles which gave off a beautiful iridescent sheen in the early morning sunlight, as she asked: "When is the funeral?"

"Tomorrow."

"I suppose I'd better come. Will Iris be there?"

"I imagine so."

She sighed. "It was really better that it ended that way."

"Yes. Petropoulos says that he would have died in great pain. While like this . . ."

"That was not what I meant." She stopped at a loose-box, over which a horse, muzzle grey and one eye sealed with a cataract (an image of the lake passed momentarily through Patrick's mind; he did not know why), was shaking his head rhythmically from side to side, and drew some sugar-lumps from her pocket. She had spoken to Patrick with the sharpness of a governess to a stupid child. "I meant it was really better for Iris. . . . Poor old boy! Poor old boy!" She held out some sugar on the palm of her hand, patting the horse as she did so. "I thought that after all these years, the thing would be over. And then you both came back, and I knew at once, even in the car, that nothing was changed. He felt exactly the same about her, and she about him. . . ." Again she scrabbled for some sugar-lumps in her pocket, and her voice, which had rung out with its usual vigorous edge when talking of her daughter and Christo, now became almost senile in its softness and sentimentality, as she cooed in a sort of baby-talk to the horse: "Poor old boy! Mummy's poor old boy! He's getting very old, izzum! Izzum! Yes, very, very old!" She turned back to Patrick: "He's twenty-seven. My husband gave him to me when we spent our three years in England. He was a wonderful jumper—I used to hunt with the Old Surrey and Burstow. I'd never hunted before and of course I've never hunted since, but I loved it, I loved every moment of it! That was something my husband couldn't understand. . . . Once, you know, I rode all the way from Salonica to Athens, alone, quite alone. My husband took the two children to Rhodes for a holiday. . . . Yes, we've been good friends, very good friends"—she sighed—"haven't we, Brendan?" She tugged one of his ears: "And now you're old, and I'm old, and our riding days are over."

To Patrick, there was pathos as well as a certain absurdity in the scene. He himself had never felt any excessive affection for an animal, and he deprecated such affection in others: caring for animals, he used to tell himself, was often a poor substitute for caring for human beings. Yet as he watched this tall, handsome, big-boned woman with her red cheeks and her white hair and her beautiful hands, heavy with their rings, growing soft and almost lachrymose as she thought of her prime, her days out hunting and her ride, extraordinary for a woman in Greece, all the way down from Salonica to Athens, something in him was touched. Yet a moment later she had forfeited that sympathy, by the matter-of-fact way in which she asked:

"I suppose Iris was terribly cut-up?"

"I suppose so."

"And she'll never forgive me." She gave a low, harsh chuckle. "Mind that puddle!" A warning hand was extended. "No, she'll never forgive me. . . . Well, in spite of that, I'm glad I saved her from that mistake."

"I'm—I'm afraid I—I don't understand." He was confused, halting and turning to her, while his shoes sank deeper and deeper into a morass of manure, sodden straw and mud, and the colour mounted to his forehead.

"When did you . . . ?"

"Have you never talked about it?"

"Never."

"What!" She was amazed. "But Iris told me that when you proposed to her, she—she made a clean breast of it all."

"No, I knew nothing. And all I know now is merely what I've guessed—no more. You'd better tell me. I shall never be able to ask Iris now." They had entered the house again as Mrs. Nicolidou said: "Iris was seventeen and Christo nineteen. They'd always been friends; Iris and Aleko—my son—never got on, and she and Christo used to do everything and go everywhere together. Christo was a great favourite with my husband. Oh, how often I told him that he would regret it—taking the boy up, and paying for him to go to the gymnasium, and allowing him to accompany us on our holidays!" She spoke with a kind of irritable disgust which seemed to embrace all the actors in her story, except of course herself. "Well, what I had always dreaded, happened. The two fell in love. I told my husband that he ought to send Christo away for ever, but he was fond of him and instead sent him to work at my son's place—the house that Iris and you now have. Fortunately, a few months later, he had to go off for his military service and then you turned up here and we thought that it had all been forgotten. But it hadn't. It never was forgotten, I see that now. . . . I never forgave Christo"—her voice had grown vibrant and harsh—"never, never. To take advantage of my husband's kindness and of his position as a servant, in that way! And Iris only seventeen at the time! It was a disgusting thing to do."

It seemed extraordinary to Patrick that this rancour should be directed against a man who had died less than two days previously. It was not in him to be jealous of a dead man—he sometimes doubted if it was in him to be jealous at all—and now, as Mrs. Nicolidou unravelled the skein for him, his only feeling was one of an almost sickening pity combined with remorse, he could not have said for what. For his own blindness, perhaps, through all these years? Or for his inability to make Iris forget that first passion? Or for his inadequacy now in the face of her grief?

"Anyway it's over. . . . And he's dead." Mrs. Nicolidou spoke with a sombre satisfaction, putting her hands in her lap and touching each of her rings in turn as if she were afraid that one might be missing. Patrick had the feeling that, in the eyes of this shrewd, domineering woman, Christo's frustrated love, his years of separation from Iris and his terrible, lonely death were all no more than what he had deserved. No doubt—to use the colloquialisms with which her talk was always scattered—he had asked for it; he had got what was coming to him.

When Patrick left the house, the sun was already high, making

his eyes ache as though from some unshed weight of tears. He
drew his dark glasses out of his pocket and slowly put them on. It
was the first time he had worn them since the drive up to the village from the harbour when he and Iris had first arrived. Walking
on, he all at once experienced an overmastering weariness which
made him wonder if he would have the strength to complete the
ten-minute climb back home. The wind that had blown all the previous day and night had now spent itself; but the pathway, winding
between two walls, was like a trough full of bruised petals and
dead leaves and dust. Yesterday he had felt remorse and an overwhelming melancholy; this morning, less than a quarter of an
hour ago, he had felt a no less overwhelming pity. Now he felt
nothing. He stooped down and picked up a handful of the refuse
in the pathway: slowly he scattered it with each dragging step he
took up and up the hill.

There was a gate, leading into a field on the right, and in the
field, so far away, he could even now see that Soula was tethering
three goats. She had a mallet in one hand and a metal pin in the
other, and bending over, she began to hammer the pin into the
ground in a sustained rhythm of vigorous stroke on stroke. Patrick
hurried: if he could pass the gate before she had finished this task,
he would escape without her seeing him. For he did not wish to be
seen; at that moment he wanted never to be seen by her again.

"*Kyrie! Kyrie* Orde!" She was shouting to him, her head raised
while she still stooped, clutching the mallet in one hand and the
pin with the other. "*Kyrie!*" He could not ignore it.

Reluctantly he went to the gate and began to walk towards her.

She grinned: "Isn't it a wonderful day? So warm. We shall soon
be able to bathe." She ran after one of the goats and grabbed at its
trailing rope: "You wicked girl!" she scolded it. She and the goat
both tugged and she called out to Patrick: "Oh, *Kyrie*, please help
me! She's so obstinate, this one. I can never get her to do what I
want." Patrick approached the animal which, as it strained away,
blinked its topaz-eyes in sleepy malevolence, at the same time
flicking a bright pink tongue around its pointed mouth.

"Oh, thank you, thank you." The goat was at last fastened. "I
didn't call you for that, but to ask you to tell the *Kyria* that I'm

sorry I shall be a few minutes late at the dispensary this morning. I have so much to do for my father—with my uncle's death, you know. . . ."

She spoke without any restraint or embarrassment or shyness, looking into his face with the large green eyes, now brilliant and now unfathomably sombre, which she had in common with her brother. Patrick glanced down at her hand which clutched the mallet: and at the sight of the blunt fingers, with their closely-cut square nails the cuticles of which were each rimmed with soil, he felt an extraordinary, violent constriction within his throat that slowly passed to leave him dizzy and weak.

Suddenly she said: "Your glasses! I thought you looked different. Are they American?"

"No, I don't think so."

"They make you look American. . . . Can I try them on?"

"If you like."

He removed them and she took them from him, eager and excited. It was pathetic, he thought, how easy it was to give pleasure to her and her brother: one allowed them to click a camera, one paid for a cake, one lent them some sun glasses. That was all that was needed.

Soula turned her head in all directions, examining the sea, the lake, the hillside behind her, the goats, the sky, the almond trees and olive trees, and then at last him. "You're green!" she exclaimed, delighted with her discovery. "They make you look green!"

He held out his hand: "Well, I must be going." Reluctantly she took off the glasses, blinking her luxuriant eyelashes in the sunlight and screwing up her face: "The sun hurts now," she said. "How funny—it hurts now. . . . Tell me, how much did they cost?"

"The glasses? Oh, about thirty thousand drachmae."

She whistled. "As much as that!"

When he reached the top of the hill where the path curved into the village, he stopped, breathless from the climb, and hands on hips, turned to gaze back. The sun had not yet caught the lake, which gleamed milky and indeterminate, like the branches of the almond trees on the misty slopes beyond it, but already the sea was covered by innumerable fine beams of light, flash upon flash, stab

upon stab. Soula was no more than a silhouette as she drew water
for the goats from a well and, straining under the weight of the
two buckets, picked her way back over the roots of the olive trees
and the tufts of asphodel and rosemary. The clink of the pails was
extraordinarily distinct as though, just behind his head, a hammer
were striking metal. All at once he felt that his eyes, in spite of
their dark glasses, could stand the glare no more; that his ears, in
spite of the distance, could no more stand that noise. Hurriedly he
walked on.

4

"It's up to you to speak to him," Iris said. "I'm far too busy. I have
to go down to the chapel this morning with the builders, and this
afternoon I promised to go and see that child who has earache."
A few days after Christo's death Iris had put in hand her scheme
for rebuilding the ruined chapel into which she had gone that day
when, seated outside, Patrick had first seen Stavro. It was outside
this chapel that Christo lay buried.

"But what can I say?"

Iris shrugged her shoulders.

"It's so much easier for you," Patrick went on. "When one
doesn't speak the language properly . . ."

"You speak Greek perfectly well."

"Anyway, he's less likely to be offended if you take him to task."

"I don't see why."

"After all, the estate *is* yours."

"But you're the man. And for a Greek it's the man—not the
wife—who is boss."

Patrick realized that there was no chance of persuading Iris to
relent: obviously it was he who must speak to Dino, she was deter-
mined on that.

All morning he put off an interview which he guessed would
be disagreeable, but after lunch when Iris had asked him "Well,
have you seen Dino yet?" he got up and said "No, I'm going now,"
and began to stroll towards the cottage. He met Stavro, coming

out of the gate, a hunk of brown bread in one hand and a clove of garlic in the other. The boy's mouth was so full that he raised the hand which clutched the piece of bread to his forehead in greeting, chewed and swallowed twice before he could say: "Hello, boss. Are you coming to the dancing?"

"Dancing? What dancing?"

"Today is the last Sunday before Lent; didn't you know that? We have a feast. Even the priests dance—it's the only day of the year when the poor b——'s are allowed to do so." He put his tongue round his teeth, made a sucking noise and swallowed again. "Perhaps I shall dance too," he grinned.

"Do you dance?"

"Sometimes. If I have enough to drink." Like most of the villagers, Stavro was, as Patrick knew, extremely abstemious; but he liked to keep up this fiction of drinking more than his parents would wish.

"Oh, by the way, I've had a letter from Typaldos and he says he's going to be here next month. He's coming on a holiday. He'll be glad to see you then, he says, and we can decide what's to be done."

Stavro grinned as he bit on the clove of garlic; his mouth full, he said: "It's awfully good of you, boss."

Embarrassed, Patrick asked: "Is your father in?"

"Yes. He's having a snooze. I'll wake him—don't go away!" Patrick had welcomed the excuse for postponing the interview; but before he could say anything, the boy put his head in at a window and shouted: "Dad! Dad! *Kyrios* Orde is here. He wants to see you."

There was a dark-red patch on one side of Dino's face, where he had been sleeping, and his top trouser-buttons and his shirt-buttons were open to reveal a grubby singlet from the neck of which a mat of coarse grey and red hair sprouted. His shoes were off; his eyelids, his voice and his movements were all heavy with sleep.

The two men sat down on straight-backed wooden chairs on either side of a square table covered with a strip of peasant-embroidery (perhaps, Patrick thought, Soula had worked it; she had given Iris such a strip as a present at Christmas). There was a smell of fresh whitewash mingling into the smell of Dino's socks, of charcoal being burned and of newly-made bread. As Patrick began to speak, not looking across at Dino who was scratching his bowed head with one of his massive hands, Patrick remembered his mother-in-law's advice: be jocular. But, though he tried over and over again, the right note would not come. Every inflection of his voice seemed to carry with it an element of falsity: now he was gushing, now condescending, now sneering, now scolding, now speaking in a tone of pettish spite and injury. He knew that each word he uttered only incensed Dino the more.

At one point Dino's wife, a thin woman with wide lips, an upturned nose and unbecomingly frizzed hair which always was worn in a net, entered bearing the traditional gifts of hospitality, a thimble of mud-like coffee and a teaspoonful of preserve: but when Patrick raised his cup and said: "To your health," only she replied, "And to your health also," Dino merely grunting as he pushed his own cup from him with a look of bitter distaste.

"Now look," he said, when Patrick had at last finished talking: the Greek put both his hands on the table before him, and Patrick noticed that they were exactly like his children's, only grossly magnified, with the same blunt fingers and the close-cut square nails each rimmed with soil under the cuticle. All at once his sluggishness had gone, his massive body was tensed as though, at a word, he would leap up to fling himself on the Englishman and his eyes, under their scowling brows, became dangerous in their fixed wooing of Patrick's nervous gaze. The Englishman had come here to insult him, he related over and over again with the same thick, choking utterance; he had spoken to him like a tramp or a thief; he had seemed to forget, as the English always forgot, the many services which his family had done for Iris and her mother through the difficult years of the war. He was not a poor man—he threw his head up proudly; he did not need the pittance which he derived from the job of bailiff. In fact, he had only agreed to do this work for them out of a feeling of loyalty to the family. He had all he wanted for his needs; and even if he hadn't, he wouldn't stoop to embezzle a million or two. He was a gentleman, as the Greeks understood that word, and even if he hadn't had a fine education, he was the equal of Patrick. The Greeks might be poor, and the

English and the Americans might despise them for that reason, but at least they had their pride—their sacred Greek pride.

Now the orator which lurks in even the humblest Greek peasant suddenly flashed out; and this man who, a moment ago, had sat slouched before Patrick like some mutely goaded ox, got to his feet, struck the table, struck his breast, gesticulated wildly and used every tone from a shout to a whisper. His wife appeared in the doorway, her arms crossed under her meagre breasts and her shoulders hunched forward as she watched him with a strange mingling of admiration for his rhetoric and indignation against this Englishman of whom she had always felt a distrust. Her mouth was slightly open as her small, green eyes shot from one of the men to the other.

It was a complete defeat for Patrick, and at the end, he found himself ignominiously pouring out apologies and excuses. He hated violence, and the sight of the Greek's brick-red, sweating face contorted with rage, of his wildly flailing arms and quivering chest and shoulders, induced in him a feeling of almost physical nausea. He capitulated: despising himself for his weakness as he did so, yet feeling, in his heart, no more responsible for that weakness than he would have done if he had screamed when suffering some excruciating agony.

When Dino opened the door for him to go, the Greek said: "Anyway you—or your wife—" he made the alternative sound deliberately insulting—"must decide whether you wish to trust me or not. We can't continue like this. Either I give up the job, or you cease to suspect me at every turn. That's flat."

"But my dear Dino, of course we don't suspect you. You've entirely misunderstood. It's just that we're—we're worried about this drop in our earnings and naturally we want to get to the bottom of the cause. We've never for one moment . . ."

"Well, that's all right then," Dino cut in grimly. Now the rage had left his face and his expression was one of exaltation, like a man's who has succeeded in at last declaring his love. "But I'm telling you straight, *Kyrie* Orde, that's the last time I want to hear that sort of talk. Next time it'll all be finished between us. Understand?"

As he walked away, Patrick's feelings of self-disgust and humiliation and anger drained away far sooner than he had expected: he,
too, experienced a strange exaltation, like the exaltation he had
seen on Dino's face, and now as he lived again through the whole
crude violence of their scene together, that exaltation became a
boundless, unreasoning euphoria.

From below the road, where a dusty square lapped round the
school, he could hear the sound of music: a drum, a clarinet, and
a fiddle played always a little sharp. Then, blending with this noise,
some ragged voices wobbled upwards, steadied themselves and, at
last acquiring confidence rang out in a triumphant unison, while
hands joined in to clap the time. From his side of the road Patrick could see nothing. A cloud of dust was rising slowly upwards,
layer upon grey layer. Remembering how Stavro had spoken of
the dancing, Patrick crossed the road and began to descend the
precipitous pathway.

The whole village seemed to be assembled and there were even
faces from other villages which Patrick had never before seen.
In the centre of the square a ring of some fifty young girls, their
hands clasped and each wearing a white kerchief over her head,
were shuffling round and round; they executed the same intricate step over and over again, the monotony of it producing in
all their faces an identical expression of sullen absorption. Within
their circle three men were dancing alone: an old shepherd, whose
small, bloodshot eyes looked out from a thicket of silver-grey bris-
tle; the owner of the café, leaping higher and higher on his short,
bandy legs, while the port-wine stain on his face seemed to darken
and throb with the exertion; and Stavro. Unlike the girls, who
were condemned to the anonymity of all performing together the
same prescribed movements, the men did as they wished, each
trying to surpass the others in the brilliance and vigour of his
inventions. Like hens, the girls jogged and shuffled round; and like
cocks the three men strutted and pirouetted for them, showing off
their plumage. As Patrick descended, he caught Stavro's eye, and
even while he was executing a phenomenal leap in the air, striking
his heels with the palm of his right hand, the boy flashed a smile.
Sweat streamed down his face and his hair was tumbled over his

forehead; he looked savage, happy, transported by the rhythm and his own accomplishment and the gasps of the onlookers.

The Englishman pushed his way through the tightly-packed crowds and, by some extraordinary accident, found himself standing next to Soula. She was leaning against the wall of the school, her bare arms crossed and her hair covered, like the hair of all the other girls, with a newly washed kerchief. She smiled and said: "Good afternoon, *Kyrie*," while her companions stared at him, then blushed, and then went into convulsions of suppressed giggling, rocking against each other and biting their lips.

"Good afternoon," Patrick returned.

"Do you like our dancing?"

"Very much."

"But you would rather watch European dancing, wouldn't you?"

"No, not at all."

"But you prefer European dancing?"

"No, I don't."

"You are saying that to please us. This dancing is only for peasants—you don't really like it. You should go to the 'Phoenix' in the town. There they do the European dancing."

The girl on her right said something in a rapid undertone to the rest of the group and their faces became even redder and their giggling even more uncontrolled.

"Actually I hate what you call 'European' dancing."

"I don't believe that. After the war, all the English soldiers wanted the European dances. I can do some of them—the 'fox'"—she used the English word—"and the waltz and the samba. But this kind of dancing"—she pointed at the dusty ring of girls—"is silly. It bores me."

As Patrick followed her gesture with his eyes, he was aware that Stavro at every leap or twirl or rhythmic stamp of the feet, never ceased to watch them. He was not smiling now, as he had smiled when he had first seen Patrick; his eyes, under their heavy brows, seemed oddly wary, intent, injured.

Closer and closer pressed the crowds. Some soldiers had now appeared, making loud remarks obviously intended for Soula's companions, punctuated by explosive bursts of laughter and thumps on each other's shoulders. A priest passed, smiling and nodding benignly as he trod on Patrick's foot, followed by a horde of ragged children who darted hither and thither emitting whistles and cat-calls. Without intending it, Patrick found himself pushed closer and closer to Soula until his right arm could feel her breast along it and his hand lay on her thigh. He tried to shift, with the movement of scurrying panic that an animal makes when a trap first closes; but already her fingers had sought out his, their two hands were linked.

He felt appalled, terrified, yet full of a boundless exhilaration. There was a tremor in his voice as he asked: "And won't you dance at all?"

Still looking straight ahead of her, she answered: "No, I couldn't, even if I wanted to. You see, we're in mourning for my uncle." Her fingers had now slipped round his wrist.

"But Stavro is dancing."

She frowned: "He shouldn't be dancing. Many people are shocked, but he says he doesn't care. It's wrong of him. I tried to stop him." She drew a handkerchief from her belt, and as she raised it to her face, tilting her head slightly towards him, she whispered: "I shall go now. . . . Follow me. . . . The dispensary."

She left, and there were a few seconds in which he decided to stay where he was; then he began to thread his way through the crowd, pushing the people impatiently to left and to right as he struggled up the pathway.

Soula was rolling some bandages when he entered; and strangely, as he smiled at her, his mind went back to the time when he had first been into this room, when it still belonged to Stavro—how long ago that seemed. She came across to him, with an extraordinary calm, and put her arms round him, and raised her lips to his. They kissed, and it was the first time they had kissed each other.

Patrick said: "We must be careful. My wife might . . ."

"She's visiting the Michaelides child. It's a three-mile walk—she can't possibly be back for another hour. I saw her go."

Patrick had forgotten this visit; and he now realized with a shock, that Soula must have been waiting and watching for her opportunity. The doubt came to him, even as she recklessly kissed him again, that perhaps, for all her youth, she was not as innocent as he had always supposed her to be; and from that thought he derived both comfort and a curious muting of his desire to possess her. Under her dress she wore nothing but a vest, hand-knitted from a coarse, unbleached wool and the roughness of this texture on the back of his hand contrasted with the smoothness of her skin on his palm. There was an odour of disinfectant in the room and it mingled with that animal-like odour of her healthy, sunburned flesh. She sighed and murmured and clung closer and closer to him.

"What was that?" He could hear a car draw up and then feet on the cobbles outside.

Soula ran to the window, pulling her dress straight: "It's her," she said. "Quick, go up the stairs into the house. You've plenty of time. If she comes in here, I'll be rolling those bandages."

Once again he was astonished by her calmness.

In the sitting-room, he had just had time to pick up *The Times* and open it at the centre page when Iris came in. "Hello," she said. She put down a basket. "Luckily I managed to get a lift back from that man in the Agricultural bank—what is his name? . . . Oh, I feel done in!" She sank into a chair, resting her head back and letting her arms dangle loose on either side.

"You do too much."

She sighed and gave that smile, compounded equally of pity and contempt, with which he seemed to have become more and more familiar in the days since Christo's death. "Oh, work is the only thing that makes the whole business tolerable!" He looked closely at her and realized, with a pang, that she had grown much thinner; that there were heavy shadows under her eyes; and that the usually resolute lines of her handsome face had begun to sag and break up into a number of fine wrinkles. "I thought you'd be down at the dancing," she said.

He wanted to get away from her now, oppressed by her pathos, his own remorse, and the frustration of never daring to share in her secret agony. "Yes, I'm just going to go," he lied. "It should be fun. Won't you come too?"

"I don't feel in the mood." She raised her dangling arms and, placing her hands in her lap, began to turn her wedding-ring round and round as she stared out of the window. She was still turning the wedding-ring when he left the room.

It seemed as if there had been no change in the square outside the school: the same shrill music, the girls shuffling exactly as they had shuffled before, the three men still leaping and twirling in the centre all gave Patrick a sensation of timelessness. This was their life, stamped out in a monotonously brutish rhythm in the dust under the olive trees. But, suddenly there was an intervention. A figure had broken the ring of girls and had pushed into the centre. It was Dino.

He hurried with an odd, stumbling run towards Stavro and catching him by the wrist began to shout at him, his voice gradually submerged by the uproar into which the crowd broke. A man next to Patrick said to his neighbour: "And quite right too!" and a woman leant over to agree: "What a shameful thing—when his uncle is barely three weeks cold!" "Disgraceful!" another woman shouted. Dino was now dragging Stavro out of the square.

Slowly the tumult spent itself: the music struck up again, the girls joined hands, and another young man took Stavro's place.

Patrick soon grew tired of watching. He could not see Soula; he felt nauseated by the smell of the bodies packed all around him; and his shoulders, his neck and the backs of his legs had all begun to ache from standing for so long in one position. He saw a gap in the crowd and wandered through it out in to a lower road which led to the café. He thought he would drink a glass of *ouzo* or of cognac.

As he strolled, hands in his pockets, he happened to look down over the parapet which separated the roadway from the falling hillside, and there, below, in an olive grove Stavro was standing, hurling his sheath knife at a tree as Patrick had seen him hurl it on that first evening of their arrival. The knife bit deep into the wood; and each time the boy then went across and began stubbornly to ease it out. All at once he glanced up.

Patrick waved: Stavro scowled, looked down at the knife, gave it another tug and then, leaving it still embedded, began to approach. He scrambled up the road, clutching at bushes and tufts of grass while stones, loosened by his boots, tumbled down the slope behind him.

"Hello, Stavro."

"Where are you going?"

"For a stroll—nowhere in particular."

"Where is Soula?" His voice sounded oddly congested.

"I don't know."

"Where did she go when you followed her?"

"Followed her?" Patrick smiled. "I didn't follow her. I went up to the house to find my wife."

The boy stared at him with a slouched, smouldering menace. "I was dancing," he said at last.

"Yes, I know. I saw you."

"No, you didn't. You hardly looked."

"I'm sorry your father stopped you."

"Anyway, it doesn't matter. I don't dance all that well." He turned his back and, hands in pockets, began to leap from tuft to tuft, foothold to foothold, down the slope. He went back to the tree and pulled out the knife. He was rubbing the blade gently up and down his palm when Patrick turned the corner and so could no more see him.

3

SPRING

I

THERE were times when Patrick feared that Iris was on the verge of
a nervous collapse. She ate little, obviously forcing herself to swal-
low mouthful after mouthful of the food placed before her, she
rarely spoke except to give an order, and she was sleeping badly.
As she went about the two tasks which now seemed to absorb all
her energies—the running of her dispensary, and the decoration
of the ruined chapel above the lake—the usual immobility of her
large features and the tonelessness of her voice seemed, in a way
that frightened Patrick, to have become those of an automaton.
Never for a moment did she slacken; spending long hours in dressing hideous sores, injecting and dosing, and then running down
to the chapel to goad the builders on. In a nearby village she had
found an old fisherman who was also a remarkable artist, and she
was employing him to cover the iconostasis. He had, Patrick discovered, been a friend of Christo.

"While I'm sleeping as badly as this," Iris said one morning, "I
wonder if you'd mind using the dressing-room?" She sat, huddled
in her dressing-gown, in a chair beside the window, and though it
was a sunny spring day, her face looked pinched and grey and cold
as she let it slip further and further forward until her chin touched
her chest.

"No, of course not." Since Christo's death they had not slept
together as husband and wife; but after the first humiliating shock,
Patrick had welcomed this privation. No longer was one image
to be perpetually superimposed on another, so much more dangerous and attractive. He felt the lines separate with a powerful
sense of release: those of the first image growing thin and faint
and drifting away; those of the second deepening, and hardening

and extending through his being, along his veins and nerves and muscles. "But look, Iris—can't you let up a little? You're far from well." Her pathos no longer filled him with a horrible, aching tenderness; it irritated him, and there was irritation in his voice when he spoke these words.

"Oh, shut up, shut up!" she cried out in a sudden, peevish exasperation. "I'm not ill. I'm all right, I'm perfectly all right." She got up from the chair, and with trembling fingers, pulled off her dressing-gown and nightclothes as she hastily began to dress. "And there's no need to stare at me like that," she suddenly added viciously.

It was soon after this that an incident occurred that served to intensify this mood of alternating despondency and irritation. Iris had been called to look at the baby of an unmarried girl who lived in a hut up on the hilltop above the village, tending goats under conditions of appalling privation and squalor, and supplementing her meagre earnings by (so it was rumoured) acting as prostitute to the soldiers in a nearby camp. The child, when Iris visited her, was tightly swaddled in rags, its body covered in a rash from their constriction. Iris ordered these filthy wrappings to be taken off and gave the mother some clothes for the child, telling her: "Of course the baby has a temperature, if you bind him up like that." But when she went back again, this time accompanied by Patrick, the baby was again swaddled.

Iris's rage was terrible: "You're a thoroughly stupid woman, and you deserve it if your child dies. Take off those rags at once! Take them off!"

The girl protested: the baby was only four weeks old, every baby of that age had to be swaddled.

"Oh, the ignorance of these people!" Iris exclaimed to Patrick. Then she picked up the child and herself began to unwrap it as though it were a badly made-up parcel. The girl rushed at her, her mouth open to display the blackened teeth of an old woman, but Iris fended her off: "Don't be silly, my girl. If you don't do what I say, it'll be easy enough to deal with you." She looked down implacably at the mother: the hut belonged to the estate. "If I come back and find this baby swaddled, I warn you—I warn you. . . . Now get me some warm water; I'm going to bathe the poor little wretch."

Two days later the village was in an uproar: the baby had died.

"Oh, I'm so tired of it," Iris said, when she had walked through the village from the chapel. "Everywhere this ignorance, this appalling ignorance! One does what one can to help them, and they look at one as if one were a murderer. The child would have died anyway, and I don't suppose the mother can have really cared a jot. But because I washed it and put it into some decent clothes, it's all my fault. I hate them—oh, how I hate them!"

Soula looked into the room: "Are you coming down to the dispensary? There are some people waiting for you."

"No, I am not! You can tell them to go away. I don't want to see them."

"But there's old Lavrachis and that——"

"Tell them to go away!"

Soula withdrew, frightened.

Iris muttered: "And it's her mother who is really at the bottom of all the fuss. I found that out."

"What do you mean?"

"Oh, she's resented my being here. Before that she was the lady bountiful of the village—her years in Athens gave her that position. Then we arrived, and her importance slowly dwindled. So, of course, she's delighted to have an opportunity to get her own back. Down at the chapel, Laros"—this was the fisherman who was covering the iconostasis—"told me that she'd even gone to the trouble of paying a call on his wife—whom she hasn't visited since last Easter—merely to run me down. But of course when she saw me in the street just now, she was all smiles and deference. Needless to say." Suddenly she went to a cupboard in which they kept glasses and drinks and poured herself some brandy: she gulped the spirit neat, and filled the glass again. "It's like a nightmare," she said.

"Don't take it so badly."

"Don't take it so badly!" she jeered back at him. "Simply because nothing ever gets under your skin, do you expect me to . . ." She broke off: "Oh, what's the use." Again she gulped: "It's the third," she said.

He was puzzled at the time by this last remark, and it was only the next day, as he pondered the whole scene, that he realized that

she must have meant that first their own child had died; then the
gipsy's in the dispensary; and now this child whom the villagers
said she had killed.

"It's the third." How stupid of him to have thought at the
time that she meant no more than that this was her third glass of
brandy.

2

PATRICK pulled off his glasses as he came out of the warmth of the
spring sunlight into the cool of the dark room, placed them on the
mantelpiece, and then drew on the coat which he had been carrying over his arm: "Hello," he said to Stavro. He went across and
looked over the boy's shoulder: "You've done that enlargement
beautifully."

The boy muttered something, then continued with the passe-
partout frame he was making.

"I've just had my first bathe of the year," Patrick said cheerfully.
As so often these last few days, he sensed an opposition in the boy's
whole stance, tone of voice and way of looking at him, and he
tried now to woo him from this mood: "The water was wonderful.
We went to that bay you told me about." Suddenly Patrick remembered that he and Stavro had once said that they would take the
first bathe of the year together, and he added, putting a hand on
his shoulder: "I wish you had been with us."

"Perhaps I would have been—if you had asked me."

"I imagined that you would have been working all afternoon."

"Oh, yes." Stavro's hands, massive and rough and yet wonderfully skilful, smoothed the passe-partout. He drew in his lower lip;
the colour had mounted under his normally pink cheeks, turning
them the same purplish-red as his father's when he was angry.
"Did you go with your wife?" he suddenly turned to ask.

"No."

"You said 'we'."

"Did I?"

"Whom did you go with?"

"With Soula. . . . Or, rather I found her down there."

"You had arranged to find her down there?"

"I don't know what you mean. Please don't speak like that, Stavro."

The boy's hands shook now as they held the finished passepartout frame: "You should be careful," he got out in a voice that sounded as if invisible fingers were pressing on his throat.

"Careful?" Patrick echoed the word, shocked by the obvious violence of the boy's emotion.

"People will talk. They're talking already." He stared at Patrick: "You're doing something dangerous. I know that in Europe men can—can do what they—they wish with girls, but here we're—we're decent people. . . ." It was extraordinary how like his father he looked as rage and indignation transfigured his features. Patrick stared, fascinated by the beauty of those flashing eyes, that trembling lower lip, those flushed cheeks and forehead, all contrasted with the clumsy inadequacy of his stammered, guttural utterance. "It's a dangerous game you're playing," the boy repeated thickly. "But—don't forget she's only fifteen. Why do you want to do it? Why—why do you?——"

Patrick, who had begun to shudder uncontrollably, suddenly, on an impulse, raised his fist and struck the boy in the mouth. "That's enough," he said. He swung round and made for the door.

He heard Stavro come after him and he expected him to retaliate with a blow. But instead the boy clutched his hand: "I'm sorry," he said. "You—you don't understand. I don't mind about—about her. . . . It's—it's you . . . you. . . . You'll only make trouble. . . ."

Patrick was hardly listening. Snatching his hand away he said: "You disgust me, all of you here—with your revolting suspicions and gossip and mischief-making." Momentarily he had forgotten those secret, shameful caresses in the cinema, in the dispensary and on the beach that very morning, as he brimmed over with righteous indignation against Stavro, against Dino and his wife, against the whole village. "Why shouldn't Soula and I be friends? She's only a child—she might be my daughter. It's only your minds—your corrupt minds . . ." He broke off.

On Stavro's face there was an extraordinary look: part agony, part shame, part exaltation. Patrick noticed that some blood was trickling out of the corner of his mouth where he had been struck.

The Englishman went out into the sunlight, and for once, although he had left his sun glasses behind, he did not notice the glare.

3

"Do hurry up! Oh, do hurry up! The car is stifling," Mrs. Nicolidou called.

"Coming!"

The old woman muttered something to herself, pushed the car door open, and then putting her fingers to the hooter, sounded peal upon peal.

"Coming, coming!" Patrick ran down the steps, taking them in twos and threes. "I'm sorry. I don't seem able to find my dark glasses. I searched all yesterday evening for them and now this morning. It's a nuisance, because today looks like a scorcher."

He climbed into the car and as he started the engine, Mrs. Nicolidou said: "I can't understand this modern mania for dark glasses. I suppose it comes from America." Most things which she did not understand or disliked she supposed to come from America. "They must weaken the eyes. I've never worn a pair in my whole life, and my sight is still as good as when I was a champion shot. You never knew that, did you?" She always showed this naïve vanity in all her achievements. "I was one of the best shots in the whole island in my day—better than my husband." She broke off: they were passing Iris's chapel, and the workmen who were straddling the holy-of-holies, hearing the noise of the car, waved their arms or caps. "Iris must be spending a lot of money on that ruin."

"It's going to look very beautiful."

"I'm not so sure about that. Why she asked that old fisherman from Cassiope to do the iconostasis is an absolute mystery to me. He's a dear old boy and his work is amusing enough, but if she had set her heart on doing the thing properly, I should have thought that someone like Zervos . . . But she's so obstinate—never listens to a thing that one tells her. . . . Oh, do be careful, do be careful! There's the bus coming."

Patrick had seen the bus already, but he repressed his irritation. "I'm worried about Iris," he said, as they jolted through a dense cloud of dust.

"Worried? Why? You mean all this religion business?"

"No. . . . I don't think she looks awfully well. Do you?"

"She looks all right. What's wrong with her?" It was astonishing that the old woman should have noticed nothing. "She's a little thinner, but she can afford to lose weight. Petropoulos was telling me that most people are far too fat. I've been thin all my life, and I've never had a serious illness. Of course she works hard. But hard work has never harmed anyone. . . . Mind out! There's a man on a donkey there!"

When they reached the town, they separated to shop and then went together to see Nazlides, the family lawyer. Although he was reputed to be rich, the trousers and jacket of his suit had a shrunken, crumpled appearance as though they had just been washed, and his black tie was frayed, and one of his shoes had a clumsy patch at the instep. He was a man of about fifty and, since the death of his young wife, the habitual expression of his face was one of a fanatical sorrow, except at those moments when he was consumed by a transitory enthusiasm for his work. In court he produced the sonorously golden tone of a great actor; but in his office he drawled and stuttered, his pointed chin sinking lower and lower on to his greasy collar, while he scribbled on his blotter or the back of a used envelope.

"I've looked through these papers. It's quite obvious that you've been cheated," he said. "And cheated on a grand scale." He looked up at Patrick with an expression of faint contempt: obviously he despised anyone who allowed himself to be cheated, particularly a foreigner.

"That's what I've been telling them ever since the man took over," said Mrs. Nicolidou. "I know all that's to be known about everyone in that village, and Dino is nothing but a crook. I've heard stories about his career in America—he was over there during prohibition, and came back with a pile." The old lady was sitting on the edge of her chair, rapping on the mahogany desk before her to emphasize certain words.

Momentarily, as she talked, Nazlides' face reassumed its expression of self-absorbed grief; then it again became keen, derisive, faintly disagreeable as he broke in: "We could make a case against him. I'm certain of that."

"No, we don't want a case," Patrick said.

"With all the evidence here—" Nazlides touched a file before him—"there should be no difficulty, no difficulty at all."

"We don't want a case."

"Then what do you want?"

"We merely want to sever all connections with him—legally." Suddenly Patrick felt a profound distaste for this whole business, combined with an irritation against his mother-in-law, against the greasy yellow face opposite him, against Iris herself. He supposed Iris was right: a halt must be called, they could not go on losing money, month after month. But it was her estate; it was for her, not him, to pay this visit and to face the scornful patronage of Nazlides who obviously regarded them both as fools to have trusted a Greek with their property.

He sat back in his chair and wearily let the old woman and the lawyer take the whole ravelled skein from his hands. Between them, they began to tug it back and forth, worrying out strand after strand, as Mrs. Nicolidou exclaimed: "And the invoice doesn't even tally!" or Nazlides, shaking his head, drawled: "It looks as if he'd just knocked off a nought or two." They both became slightly flushed, and neither of them remembered to drink the coffee which the secretary had placed before them.

"Then these fishing-rights—these fishing-rights, Mr. Orde— these fishing-rights on the lake," Nazlides all at once roused Patrick. "There's something wrong there. Five million for a year, it's an absurd sum. Absolutely absurd. Lazzari who has rights on a part of the lake at Kanoni tells me that he pays five times that."

"What did I say?" Mrs. Nicolidou demanded of Patrick. "Didn't I say to Iris?" She leant across the desk, once again rapping with her fingers for emphasis as she told the lawyer: "That man is owed money by most of the village. They were all in debt to him after the failure of the olive crop two years ago. And so they do exactly what he tells them. There's not one of them who would dare to bid against him when the rights go up for auction."

"The answer to that is to get an outsider to rent the rights." Nazlides paused, shading in an oval he had scribbled on the envelope before him. "Lazzari, for example."

Patrick remembered that Nazlides' dead wife had been a cousin of this Lazzari and the suspicion passed through his mind that perhaps the two men had between them come to some "arrangement": in Greece one could never be sure.

Once again he leant back in his chair, he felt his eyelids drooping. Really, he no longer cared; what did it matter?

When they were leaving and he was shaking the lawyer's peculiarly cold, moist hand, Nazlides said: "Well, I think that'll all go smoothly. But, you know, Mr. Orde, this should be a lesson to you. In Greece, unless one knows as much about one's business as your mother-in-law here"—he and the old woman exchanged gratified smiles—"it's always far better to do everything through a lawyer. That is why there are so many lawyers in the country—almost as many lawyers as government regulations! . . . No, I am not saying that as an advertisement for myself or because I want you to employ me; I am busy enough as it is—yesterday I worked thirteen hours. But a man without a lawyer in Greece is like a ship without a rudder."

After the gloom of the office, the sun in the square was an agony to Patrick. The vast dusty expanse on which in the morning soldiers were drilled, in the afternoon children played football, and in the evening lovers strolled together, now at midday stretched deserted under its tattered acacias and poplars like a lake of salt. The pillars of the arcade, shimmering through the heat-haze, seemed to be about to buckle and dissolve. Yet it was still only March.

"I must buy myself another pair of dark glasses. Can you wait a moment?"

"Goodness, how extravagant!"

"I can't stand this glare."

Mrs. Nicolidou was about to protest at the delay in getting home when she saw the Harbourmaster and Dr. Petropoulos seated at a table outside "Caprice"; the same table at which Stavro and Soula had sat that evening of the cinema. "Oh, there's Petropoulos!" she exclaimed. "I shall go and drink an orange-squash with him. I so like to tease him—such a serious young man!"

Although Patrick had never been into the optician's before, the proprietor addressed him by name; he supposed that by now he was known all over the island as the husband of Iris. He was an obsequious youth who insisted on speaking English: "These are very chic . . . very snob . . ." He went behind Patrick and himself drew on the glasses. They were of a kind Patrick had never seen before, transparent to the wearer but presenting to the onlooker what appeared to be two elliptical mirrors set in steel frames.

"Look in the glass, please," the young man now commanded.

Patrick looked: then he leant forward, peering closer and closer. Fascinated, he pursued the image of his face back and forth, back and forth, as it was thrown, ever-diminishing, from the lenses on his eyes to the mirror before him, until at last becoming infinitesimal, it vanished from sight.

There was a silence; the young man tapped his foot.

"I'll take these," Patrick said.

"Very chic," the young man repeated. "Shall I wrap them up?"

"No, I shall wear them."

Patrick sat down between the Harbourmaster and the Doctor, and he thought of how small children covered their eyes with their hands and said: "You can't see me now." Irrationally, he felt the same thing. As he talked, they looked at him: he could see them, but all they could see were tiny reflections of themselves wriggling over the places where his eyes should have been. He smiled to himself.

"What a vulgar pair of glasses!" Mrs. Nicolidou suddenly turned to exclaim. "Where on earth did you get them?"

"I think they're rather fun."

"They're utterly revolting!"

As they left the town a khaki-clad figure thumbed them for a lift. "Shall we? Shan't we?" Patrick asked; he drew up and then realized, with a shock, that it was the officer who had sat behind Soula in the cinema. He at once wished he had not stopped.

The young man appeared to hesitate before he loped across the road, put his head in at the window and said the name of their village.

"Yes. Get in," Patrick said.

"Veloudios," the young man said. "Veloudios," he repeated the name as he thrust his arm in turn at them. Grunting, he placed himself on the edge of the back seat, holding his cap between his knees in both his pink hands. Patrick noticed that the rim of the cap had left a plum-coloured weal across his wide forehead.

There was a silence until he said: "Is this a Rolls Royce?"

"Yes."

"They're supposed to be the best English cars?"

"Yes."

"I prefer American cars. . . . Of course this car is old, isn't it?"

"Twenty-six years. No American car would stand up to these roads for half that time."

"Why don't you get a new car?"

"Because we like this one."

Patrick felt riled by the young man's questions; but he reminded himself that the majority of these cadet-officers came, not from the towns, but the villages, and that what appeared to be impoliteness was probably merely a rusticity of manner.

There was another silence which Mrs. Nicolidou at last broke. "Why are you going to our village?" she asked. "Do you know someone there?"

Patrick had wanted to put the same question; but not being a Greek, he had shrunk from seeming inquisitive.

Veloudios turned his cap round in his hands, examining its sweat-stained lining. "Didn't you know? We are camping nearby. For two weeks. . . . I had to go into the town to see a dentist," he added. "I have good teeth; this is the first that has ever been stopped." He tapped one of his eye-teeth with his forefinger. "He wanted to give me an injection, but I don't like all that nonsense."

"What *village* are you from?" Mrs. Nicolidou asked disdainfully, not bothering to turn her head round as she spoke.

"I'm not from a village. I'm from Cymae."

"Well, that's almost a village!" She laughed and the young man flushed in annoyance. "Isn't it?"

None of them spoke again until they left Veloudios at a bend outside the village and he muttered his thanks. "The conceit!" Mrs. Nicolidou exclaimed as, hands in pockets, he hastened down a pathway.

Patrick had also felt that the young man was conceited; but now as Mrs. Nicolidou went on to criticize the provincial peculiarities of his speech, the lengths to which he grew the nails of his little fingers and the smell of cheap eau-de-Cologne which still clung to the car, his sympathy veered away from this snobbery and hung poised above them lacking a direction.

Patrick left Mrs. Nicolidou at her house and then, with a curious sense of aimlessness combined with fatigue, he drove back home. He could still taste the dust of the journey, and his eyes still smarted with it. Under his coat, his silk shirt was sticky. His shoes felt too small for him.

On an impulse he ran in, fetched his bathing things and camera, and made for the beach. As he passed the cottage on his way down, he saw Stavro at work in the small garden, planting some celery.

Patrick had not spoken to the boy since that scene, the evening before, in the dark-room, but now on an impulse he shouted out: "Come and have a bathe."

Stavro looked up; then he glanced down at the trench at which he had been working and Patrick assumed that he was going to ignore him out of pique and injured feeling. But once more he looked up, and now he was grinning: "Wish I could. I've got this job to do."

"Leave it!"

"And what will my father say?" Suddenly, he jumped to his feet and began to dust the mud off his knees and hands. "Oh, b—— my father," he said. "I'll come."

As they hastened down the path, it seemed to Patrick as if all the events of the previous evening must, in some extraordinary way, have passed from the boy's memory. He joked and laughed and teased Patrick as he always liked to do, putting an arm round his shoulder to show that no offence was meant. The Greeks, Patrick realized, are a magnanimous race, and though they are swift to resent an injury, they are no less swift to forget. Yet there, at the corner of Stavro's mouth, was the reminder of all that had happened—a darkening bruise which gave to his face a not unattractive asymmetry.

Stavro pulled off his sweat-stained clothes. Like most of the Corfiote peasants, and unlike his sister, he did not bother about personal cleanliness: probably, Patrick decided, it was only when he swam that he ever immersed himself in water. He stripped himself with an unselfconscious grace and then waited, his hands on his hips and his legs wide apart, for Patrick who was still fiddling with his bathing-trunks.

"Are those nylon?" he asked.

"Yes."

"From America?"

Just as Mrs. Nicolidou believed that everything undesirable came from America, so Stavro believed that everything desirable must come from there.

"No. From Italy."

"And how do you like my bathing-trunks?" he joked, flicking at the frayed elastic which held up his grey cotton underpants. "They're smart, aren't they?"

"Very smart. . . . So smart that I'm going to photograph you in them."

Stavro at once assumed a pose, crossing his arms and tensing all the muscles in his legs, neck and shoulders. He scowled at the lens, his face appearing all at once brutish and savage.

"Oh, don't look like that!" Patrick laughed. "Relax—please relax."

"What a pity there's no one here to photograph us together. Do you realize it has never been done?"

Patrick was soon tired by swimming and he came in from the water, lay down on the sand and put on his dark glasses. Stavro, who was a wonderful swimmer, did not join him until nearly half an hour afterwards. Smiling, breathless and dripping with water, he flung himself, face downwards, on the sand beside the English-man. "What energy," Patrick said. "You make me feel so old. . . . I do love this place," he added.

It was a small beach, shaped like a half-moon, with hillocks rising behind it, covered in olive trees, clumps of asphodel and a broom that gave off an odour of turpentine.

"And there's never anyone here," Stavro murmured, his fore-head resting on his crossed arms. "I used to come here with my Danish friend—he could swim even better than I can. He could swim under water from that rock"—he turned his body to point— "to that one over there. Wonderful! He was a boxer too. We were good friends." He looked down at his hand, as he let sand trickle over the fingers. "But I like you much better." Patrick said nothing, and a moment later the boy exclaimed: "You're wearing some different dark glasses! I've only noticed them this minute."

"Yes. I bought them in town this morning."

"You bought them this morning!"

"I've lost my other pair."

"But how silly of you! I've got them."

"*You've* got them?"

"Yes, I found them just before you came back in—in the courtyard."

"In the courtyard? How did they get there? I suppose I must have dropped them."

"I've got them in my pocket." He began to turn out his trousers and then said: "No, I must have left them at home. . . . But why on earth did you buy some new ones? Though these are much nicer." He leant over Patrick, gazing down at the twin reflections of his own face, and bare throat and shoulders as he murmured in wonder: "But how do they work? I can see my own self." He touched each of the lenses in turn with his forefinger. "They're marvellous. I can see myself, and yet you can see me."

Patrick laughed; but Stavro continued seriously: "Yes, I much prefer them to the other pair." Fascinated, he went on staring for several seconds into Patrick's eyes until the Englishman sat up and said: "Well, I suppose we should make for home." That scrutiny, combined with the proximity of the boy's body to his, had filled him with a curious shrinking unease. He supposed it was because the brother was so like his sister.

When they passed the cottage on their way home, Stavro said: "If you wait a moment, I'll slip in and fetch your glasses."

"Another time."

"No, I'll get them now."

As Patrick stood at the gate, not wishing to be seen by Dino, he all at once heard the boy's and his father's voices raised in some altercation. He supposed that Dino was angry because Stavro had left his work, and Patrick knew that he ought to intervene and say it was his fault for having persuaded the boy to do so. But he remained where he was: soon there would come what Mrs. Nicolidou had called a "show-down" with Dino—as soon, Patrick knew, as the lawyer's letter arrived—but he dreaded that show-down, as he dreaded every unpleasantness, and had no wish to hasten it.

"Hello. Are you waiting for someone?"

"Hello, Soula."

The goats which she was leading tugged her away from him, but she managed to drag them back as she said: "It sounds as if Stavro and father were at it again."

"It's my fault, I'm afraid. I persuaded Stavro to knock off work and come for a bathe with me."

She stared at him and exclaimed: "You have some new dark glasses!"

Patrick told her how he had come to buy them.

She, too, like Stavro, peered at her own reflection in the lenses. "But can you see through them?"

Patrick laughed. "Of course."

"May I try them?"

He gave the glasses to her.

When she handed them back, she said: "I think I prefer the others." Once again the goats tugged her away, and as Patrick watched her, with her small white teeth clenched, her bare arms and legs straining with her effort to control the animals, he experienced a swift and ferocious renewal of desire.

Stavro came out through the garden: "Here they are!"

"Thank you, Stavro. . . . Now I have two pairs." As Patrick

looked up at the Greek girl, her ankles and bare feet grey with the dust of the roadway, her hair tousled and the back of her right hand crossed with a scar-like weal where the rope had cut deep, he wanted to make some offering, however valueless and absurd, to her health and youth and beauty. "Would you like these?" he asked.

"Me?" she was astonished.

"I don't want two pairs—what can I do with two? And these are so much grander . . . so take the others, please."

Reluctantly she took them: her acceptance filling him with an extraordinary calm which came like a muffled echo of a calm he had only known before after making love to Iris in the first months of their marriage. She did not say thank you, for she was too embarrassed to do so, and her eyes were averted.

Stavro was staring at him, both hands clutching the iron spikes of the gate as he swung it between them.

"Now I must go. I want to develop these photographs I've just taken." Patrick patted his camera-case. "Good-bye."

"Good-bye," Soula said. Stavro said nothing. He was scowling, his lips drawn back slightly, as though he had just tasted something bitter.

When Patrick reached the dark-room he took off his sun glasses and went over to the mantelpiece to leave them there. It was as he crossed the floor, the glasses in his hands, that he remembered, with a curious shock as of two invisible objects colliding within him, how yesterday he had performed exactly this same action. But yesterday Stavro had been watching. "I do steal things, you know." The words came back, exactly as Stavro had spoken them, with a subdued, taunting irony. Transfixed, Patrick stood with his own white face reflected up at him from the lenses in his hands.

4

"Won't you join us, Stavro?"

"No, I'm far too busy." The answer came as a kind of sullen growl. "What a life! It's already half-past six." He raised his pick and hacked again at the soil.

"Is something the matter with Stavro? Is he annoyed about something?"

"I don't know," Soula replied, nervously fiddling with the rolled bundle which contained her bathing-costume and towel, as she went down the hill before him. "I don't think so."

"He's behaving so oddly? You must have noticed it. And last night he was going to come and help me with some enlarging and he never came."

"He *was* annoyed last night," Soula admitted slowly. "But he's never annoyed for long."

"What was he annoyed about?"

"Oh, these dark glasses." She put a hand to them. "You should have given them to him."

"But I wanted to give them to you."

"You see, it was he who found them. Just as it was he who was first your friend," Soula added with what appeared to Patrick to be irrelevance.

"Never mind. I'll buy him a pair when I'm next in town."

"That won't be the same."

"Why not?"

Soula shrugged her shoulders. "I don't think he would think it was the same."

"He's very fond of you."

"Of me!" She laughed: "That's what you know."

"I think he's fonder of you than of anyone else in the world."

"Nonsense! . . . He's fond of *you*—that's quite obvious."

A woman working in a field with a hoe, a khaki-coloured rag wound round her head, looked up at them as they passed, and Soula blushed and said: "We ought to have come separately."

"Why?"

"People talk. They've begun talking about us." She turned, smiling, as she waited for him to catch up with her at the bottom of the slope: Patrick never ceased to be amazed by her nimbleness. "I don't mind. They've talked about me before."

"Before?"

"Oh, unless a girl says nothing and stays at home all day, they always begin to gossip."

"But you're only fifteen."

"What does that matter? I'm already a woman—aren't I?" There was something horrifying and yet infinitely exciting to Patrick in the suggestive precocity with which she spoke that last sentence.

"Yes, you're already a woman." With a sudden reckless ardour he tried to put an arm round her, but she pulled free and ran from him, calling: "Wait, wait, wait!" as she jumped from one rock or tuft to another, swiftly down towards the half-moon of olive-coloured sand. Once again she turned, smiling, as she waited for him.

"You must be careful," she warned. "One can be seen from the top of that slope. It's not for myself—but you."

"Oh, I don't care." Nor, at that moment, did he care; for the first time in his life he was experiencing that utter heedlessness, a kind of insanity, which accompanies only the extremes of lust or love.

Once again the events of the previous day were repeated; they stripped, they bathed, and Soula, like Stavro, remained in the water long after Patrick had left it. She even flung herself down, in exactly the same position, and in exactly the same spot, as Stavro the day before. Strangely, too, as her head was pillowed, forehead downwards, on her crossed arms, her brown body, gleaming with large drops of water, might almost have been her brother's in its youthful strength, its litheness, its grace. Yet, though the hour and the glittering water and the curved sky and the olive-coloured slopes were all still the same, yet all seemed subtly different. Like a different light, radiating from his body to modify and obscure the light from the sun, Patrick felt his desire intangibly merging into everything, covering everything, changing everything. It was a frightening process.

When Soula had stripped, her back turned to him, and had pulled on her costume (it was black and in one piece, cut high at the neck and with a small skirt) he saw her remove something dangling from the end of a bootlace round her neck and stuff it into the pocket of her dress where she had already placed her dark glasses. He would have thought nothing of it—after all, Greek peasants nearly all carried holy medallions or charms—had it not been for the curiously furtive way in which she had performed the action. Could it be that she was ashamed of appearing superstitious? He knew how anxious both she and Stavro were to seem "European" in his eyes.

Yet curiosity and a vague suspicion still persisted; so that when he was alone on the beach and she was swimming far into the distance towards the mountains of Albania, he pulled the dress towards him and tugged at the end of the bootlace dangling from the pocket.

The object was a brass army-button, stamped with the crest and motto of the cadet-school in the town. Patrick turned this odd keepsake over and over in his palm; then he replaced it.

When Soula had come out of the water and was lying beside him, he asked her: "What is that thing you wear round your neck?"

"What thing?" Her voice was sleepy and muffled.

"When you took off your dress, I noticed you had something round your neck. I couldn't see what it was."

"Oh, that!" There was a pause: "It's one of these charms. To keep off the evil-eye. I expect you think that funny, don't you? You don't believe in the evil-eye."

"Where did you get it from?"

"Oh, I don't know," she now spoke almost fretfully. "Someone gave it to me. I can't remember who."

Patrick had a curiously vivid recollection of a cap, its lining stained with sweat, being turned round and round between a pair of pink, fleshy hands. When he lowered his eyelids, it seemed that he could see the outline of the cap imprinted on them, black on red. Then, opening his eyes again, he remembered the cap above a face, a face stupid yet not unhandsome, with small blue eyes, a blond moustache and lips almost girlish in their fullness and moistness. There was a badge on the cap, stamped with a crest and motto.

He felt Soula's hand, the palm grained with sand, slip into his: "What are you thinking?" she asked.

"Nothing." With an effort he blinked away the image on his eyelids. "And you?"

"I was thinking how I would like to go to Europe. How I would like to be rich. How I would like to dress in beautiful clothes. How

I would like to have my hair permed, and grow my nails long. How I would like to be married—to a man like you." Once again her palm rested on his; then her fingers caressed his wrist.

Somewhere, out there, the curving beach lost itself in an intolerable glitter, as though the sun were fretting on the edge of a sickle; and out there that image of suspicion shrivelled, flared and was also soon lost, disintegrating into a dust as scorching as the sand which burned beneath it. Everything grew incandescent, melted, merged: their bodies into the sand, the sand into the dust, the dust into the air. They felt themselves blown hither and thither on stray gusts of passion.

"Not here, not here," Soula said. "Anyone might see us."

She pulled free from him and stood up, and reluctant and dizzy Patrick stood up beside her. Then she took his hand and led him like a blind man, stumbling behind her, over the glittering sand.

Here, round the point of the ridge, the hills had collapsed half-heartedly into a cliff, neither sheer nor exalted, its surface an ultramarine colour blotched with rust. Bushes, and even trees, clung to the sides and tufts of a coarse saxifrage whose flowers had the sour-sharp smell of mouldy bread.

"Here we're safe."

Now they were in the shade with a great rock like a jet bubble over them. Soula took his hand and inserted it into the high neck of her bathing-costume; she gave a curious animal-like grunt when his fingers touched her nipple, and then rolled away from him, covering her face in her hands, and drawing her knees up.

"What's the matter?"

"It's so useless."

"Useless?"

"You're married. You don't really care for me. What's the good?" She spoke with a kind of peevish exasperation and he knew that she was right: what was the good? These moments with her were a kind of insanity; but he did not wish his life to be a prolonged insanity. He said nothing, staring up into the blankness of the rock which was not really jet, as he had first thought it after the glare, but dark-green and purple and the deepest of red, the colours interveining each other with a wonderful intricacy.

All at once Soula had thrown herself upon him. "Anyway, what does it matter? What does it matter?" she demanded in a desperate ardour. "I don't care."

They might almost have been fighting each other. Somewhere high above the cliff, goat-bells tinkled restively; a dead leaf detaching itself from a stunted oak, circled slowly down and down, until it alighted on the sand, looking now, dark brown on beige, like nothing more than a footmark or a place where some water had dripped.

"What was that?"

A shower of stones pattered about them: as they both jerked up, their faces, streaked with sweat, still looked dazed and dreamy although their bodies were tense. They stared at each other, as if in mutual accusation.

"It was Stavro," Soula said at last.

"How do you know?"

"I saw him for a moment. He was up there on the rock—he must have been watching us."

Patrick got to his feet: "Stavro!" he shouted. "Stavro!" After lying flat for so long, he felt vaguely giddy as the blood thumped through his brain. He put his hands to his mouth: "Stavro! Stavro!"

An echo; a tinkle of goat-bells; silence.

"He's gone," Soula said.

"Will he tell your father?"

She shrugged her shoulders. "Perhaps."

The apathy with which she spoke the one word as she slowly drew up the shoulder-straps of her costume caused him a violent irritation: "You must stop him saying anything," he said.

"If I can." She was rubbing a birth-mark on her shoulder with one forefinger as though she imagined that in this way she would be able to erase it.

"Do you think he came down here purposely to spy on us?"

"Of course."

"What will your father do if he knows?"

Again she shrugged her shoulders.

"Anyway, we haven't done"—he hesitated, embarrassed—"we

haven't done anything, really. That's fortunate. In Greece you lay so much importance on that."

"Would you—would you have done anything but for—but for Stavro?"

"Perhaps."

She sighed and came over to him again and put her firm brown arms round him and pressed her breasts close to his chest. After she had kissed him she said: "I thought the English were cold."

"You were wrong."

She seemed curiously unruffled that Stavro should have seen them, as she walked, ahead of him, back to the beach where their clothes were lying, and he began to persuade himself that, since she knew Stavro much better than he did, there could obviously be no reason for alarm. The boy hated his father so much, after all, and would be unlikely to wish to betray anyone to him.

Soula once again turned her back as, having pulled her bathing costume down over her shoulders she slipped her keepsake, the button on the bootlace, over her head. Patrick watched her, his arms inserted into his shirt as he prepared to put it on; then he turned to look out towards the sea, buffeted hither and thither by cross-currents of suspicion, remorse, terror. He scrabbled into his clothes; after lying for so long in the sun, even his silk shirt felt as rough and hot on his skin as though it were coarse flannel. "We had better go back separately," he said.

She had put on the dark glasses he had given her, and now once again she looked about her at the sun, the sand, the trees, his face and even her own fingers, lost in a childish wonder as she repeated: "Yes, we'd better go separately."

On the way home, Patrick became suddenly conscious that Stavro was trailing behind him. The boy remained always some hundred yards away, and if Patrick halted he would halt too. Once Patrick began to walk back and then the boy himself retreated. Patrick wanted to shout out: "What do you want? Why are you following me?" but he knew that would be folly, since there were peasants working all round them in the fields. He tried to imagine what the boy must now be feeling: rage, of course, and jealousy, and disgust and the wish for revenge. And, willing himself into

Stavro's personality, he all at once achieved an empathy rare for a man usually so obtuse about the feelings of others, and he found himself experiencing an extraordinary burning pity which all but persuaded him, against all reason, to go back to the boy, to demand pardon of him, to take his hand, to make some assertion of affection and reconciliation.

Anna, the maid, ran out to him as he came into the house, shadowy with its lowered Venetian blinds: "I don't know what's the matter with the mistress. She's been lying on her bed all afternoon. I took her some tea and she told me to take it away. She was crying."

"I'll go up and see her."

Patrick went into their bedroom. "Iris," he called softly through the gloom. Then, as his eyes grew accustomed to this muting of light, he saw the curious animal-like shape huddled up in one corner of the bed with the sheet drawn over it. "Iris! What's the matter?"

There was no reply: until suddenly the shape began to rock convulsively from side to side with long, dry gulping sobs that sounded not unlike some terrible spasm of choking.

He went to her, and pulled the sheet away, revealing a disorder of tumbled black hair, creased underclothes and limbs twisted about with bedclothes.

"What is it?" he said. "What is it?"

She snatched the sheet from him and once again drew it over her head. He tried to ease her away from the wall, into his arms, but she struggled free from him, sobbing out: "Leave me alone! Leave me! Leave me!" on a single desperate note.

"Iris . . . oh, Iris," he said. He was appalled.

Suddenly she sat up. Her cheeks were white and blotched with tears and he saw that in one hand she was clutching something which he thought was a small photograph. "You're so good," she gulped out. "So kind . . . always so kind . . . and I—I've behaved so . . . so badly . . ." Once again she threw herself on to the bed in a paroxysm of weeping.

"Don't be silly," he said. "What's the matter with you? What's happened?"

He waited for her to control herself.

"I don't know . . . I can't stop . . ." The words seemed to come, not from her throat, but from somewhere deep inside herself, jerked out in agonized spasm after spasm. "I loved him so! I loved him so!" Suddenly, she put whatever she was clutching in her hand up to her lips as though, by this frantic action, she could somehow push back into silence the words which must already have reached him.

Patrick took the raised hand in his, and eased the fingers open: the photograph—for photograph it was—fell lightly on the eider-down. He looked down at it. It had been cut from a strip of contact prints which he himself had thrown away a month ago when clearing up his dark-room, and it showed Christo standing by the Rolls-Royce. It was not a good photograph because, still unused to the Greek light, Patrick had over-exposed it: yet the very absence of any sharp contrast between dark and light gave to the thin, unsmiling figure standing beside the ramshackle hearse of a car a curious, almost ghostlike quality, the outlines of his body merging into the hazy outlines of the landscape beyond.

"Now you know," she said quietly: all at once she was speaking in her normal voice.

"But I knew all along."

"You knew!"

"Yes."

"And you said nothing!"

"What was the point? I only knew after his death."

Suddenly she clung to him gripping his arms savagely with her powerful hands, and pressing her cheek against his own. "Forgive me, forgive me, forgive me," she cried out over and over again. "I couldn't help it. I couldn't help it. For all those years—all those years . . ."

"It doesn't matter," he said.

He was wonderfully gentle with her, running his fingers through her hair to smooth it away from her forehead and then taking a handkerchief and wiping her tears away. He kissed her, as she lay, still crying softly in his arms, over and over again on her forehead and her moist cheeks and her hair. He felt a terrible pity for her, compared to which the pity he had felt for Stavro less than an hour ago was no more than the first twinge of pain that precedes a violent toothache; and he felt a hopeless inadequacy, and a sadness, and a strange kind of envy. She had loved someone as he would never love anyone: through years of separation and loneliness and silence, and now through death. Whereas he . . . He thought of Soula and of how he had peeled the bathing costume down to her narrow waist, and he asked himself if for her he could ever know the same devotion: and he knew that he could not.

He went on with his task of comforting the woman who lay, sobbing like a beaten child, on the darkened bed beside him. Nor did it once occur to him that by telling her about the events of that afternoon he might perhaps be able to appease some small part of the agony of her guilt.

5

"I don't know what's the meaning of this!"

Dino strode into the room, his hat on the back of his head, and thrust a letter out at Patrick. He was quivering with rage, his face shining crimson and meaty.

Patrick glanced at the letter: "Doesn't it speak for itself?"

"Speak for itself!"

"It's obvious that this arrangement between us has not worked out well. With Christo it was—different."

"Different!" Like many men who are not quick-witted Dino's repartee consisted chiefly in the angry or contemptuous repetition of some word or phrase already spoken. "Oh, it was different all right!" There was a peculiar vulgarity in the jeering manner in which he got out this last sentence and Patrick wondered if he had known about Christo and Iris; he supposed that he had.

"We saw Nazlides last week and he agreed that something was amiss. So we asked him to terminate your employment with us. That's all there is to it. If you wish to discuss anything, you must discuss it with him. The matter is entirely in his hands." The sentences were short, clipped, over-precise from a desire to conceal nervousness. Patrick began to fiddle with the papers before him. "So it's no use coming here. If you have anything to discuss——"

"I have something to discuss! With you!" Dino pulled a chair from the wall and thrust it towards the desk. He sat down. "Then you can decide whether you want lawyers or not."

"Look here, Dino, I've told you——" Patrick began to rise.

"I should listen, *Kyrie*, if I were you." The voice had a curious, slurred menace: "I should listen. I should sit and listen."

Patrick sat down. Outside a bell was tolling for one of the innumerable services held during Holy Week.

"Aren't you being a little stupid?" Dino said. "Do you want to make an enemy of me?" As he spoke he tugged at the coarse hair which sprouted out of his open collar. He stared at Patrick, his gaze curiously sleepy and ruminative, and Patrick stared back. Suddenly he smiled: "So you want to get rid of me? And you want to terminate my contract for the fishing-rights on the lake? That's the idea, is it? Is it?" Patrick did not answer. Outside the bells scrambled and jostled together, in tinny confusion; Iris was there, almost the whole village would be there. Patrick put a hand to his forehead and felt it cold and moist.

"Well, there are some things you should have thought of first. My daughter, for instance. You know whom I mean, don't you?" The irony was crude. "Soula—my daughter. You should have thought of her first." In a sudden choking fury he banged the desk and cried: "People are sent to prison for three years—four years—five years— for doing what you've done! And by God, I'll—I'll . . ." Incoherent now, his hand continued to beat the desk as tears of rage formed at the corners of his eyes.

"I've done nothing to your daughter. I've kissed her, yes—I may even have made a little love to her." Patrick was aware, all at once, that the bells had stopped: but the air still seemed to be churning with their vibrations. "She's still—still a virgin, so I can't possibly see——"

"A virgin! Still a virgin! You—you bloody liar!" Dino had leapt to his feet and there was a moment when Patrick thought that the Greek was about to fling himself upon him. Making a wide, straggling gesture with his arms, Dino shouted: "So you

think you can get away with it by denying it all! I've got all the
evidence I want—all the evidence a court would want! A girl of
fifteen . . . and you married, a married man . . . an innocent girl
. . . who probably didn't even understand what filthy things you
were doing to her . . ." Once again tears of rage formed in the
corners of his eyes and a large vein throbbed down one side of his
throat as the words were choked out of him. "Well, we'll see—
we'll see! . . . And then you have the bloody cheek to accuse me of
being crooked! You English are all alike—hypocrites, hypocrites!"
Suddenly he pointed a finger at Patrick, leaning over the desk so
that his face, flushed and damp with sweat, was below the Englishman's and his bloodshot eyes were glaring up at him. "Now I'm
telling you straight. Unless I hear from this—this Nazlides"—his
forefinger stubbed at the letter between them—"that I'm to disregard all this, you'll be getting a letter yourself—from *my* lawyer.
Understand? Understand? You've got till next Tuesday to decide
how you want it to be. But I shouldn't make an enemy out of
me, boss—I shouldn't make an enemy out of me." He went to the
door and pulled it open: "My children tell me everything," he said.
He smiled: "Everything." Then he was gone.

Patrick sank back into his chair; all at once he felt faint and
sick, as though he had just witnessed an accident. He shut his eyes
and drew his trembling hands over them. So Stavro had spoken! It
had been silly of him to expect anything else. For a moment, defi-
ance flared in him—he would fight them; he would refuse to be
blackmailed, he would spend his last penny before he gave in—and
then died out. A Greek court would always be prejudiced against
a rich foreigner in favour of a poor Greek. And then there was Iris
. . . And, anyway, how could they go on living in the village after
such a scandal? He had been reckless, madly reckless; and the fact
that, technically, he had done nothing to Soula that was forbid-
den by Greek law, mattered hardly at all. Probably she wasn't a
virgin anyway. And he all at once thought of the button dangling
between her naked breasts. . . .

He walked out aimlessly on to the verandah and, looking
down, saw that Iris was approaching up the road from the chapel
with slow, dragging steps, her lowered head turned rapidly from

side to side as though she were looking for something she had lost. He descended to meet her:

"Is the service over?"

"No, not yet. I had enough." She began to climb the steps ahead of him, with that same curious lowering and shifting of the head from side to side; then she turned: "It doesn't seem to mean anything more to me." Her voice was flat and toneless.

"What doesn't mean anything more to you?"

"All the things that I used once to believe. They mean nothing. Nothing." She stood in the doorway leading into the sitting-room and peered down at the lake; its cataract-like surface seemed to have hardened into a number of greyish-blue ridges as though some surgical instrument had prodded it a little sideways and then let it be. She looked round at him with a kind of bewildered panic: "Nothing seems to mean anything any longer," she said.

He went to her and put his arm round her, forgetting the fear and remorse and humiliation of the last hour with Dino, in his pity for her. "That happens from time to time," he said. "Don't worry. Don't worry, darling."

"It's as if—as if something had happened to life at the source. I don't know. I can't explain." Suddenly she threw her arms round him: "Let's get away from here! Let's go! Let's go at once!"

6

PATRICK had forgotten his camera, and Iris and Mrs. Nicolidou sat waiting for him in the car as he ran up the stairs, two and three at a time, into the dark-room to fetch it. A number of villagers had appeared to see them leave, but none of them would come near the car, and they would only look at the two women when they knew that the women were looking elsewhere. It was Easter Saturday and there was no work for the day.

It was unusually hot in the dark-room for while he had been sorting and packing there Patrick had had the shutters opened and the curtains taken down, so that now the early morning sun streamed in on chipped enamel basins and trays and rows of half-empty bottles. He had not packed all his equipment: he and Iris were going away for a month or for two months; then they would come back. This was what they had told the servants, and this was even what they had told each other. They almost believed it.

He picked up the camera and then, suddenly, on an impulse, began to open the back: inside were the photographs of the last weeks—of Soula and Stavro with the goats, on the terrace, by the sea, their arms round each other, their legs bare, their teeth gleaming white out of their brown faces as they both smiled at him. . . . The light enfolded them; they were dissolved. For, hurriedly, on an impulse, he had begun tugging the film, cold and sleek on his agitated fingers, out from its cassette, and frame by frame allowed the light to devour it. At last he had finished; and the unravelled spool lay on the floor, like a coiled ribbon of steel in a shaft of sunlight from the window. Gazing down at it, he experienced a miraculous sense of freedom.

When he began to descend again, the camera held between both his hands, he suddenly thought, he could not say why, of that evening when he had wandered out one dusk to find Dino whipping Stavro while Soula looked on. There had been a bat—or was it a bird?—swooping overhead, and the shadows, like the shadows now, had seemed to sway from side to side of the courtyard as though it were a tank, splashing against the walls and then clotting there like blood. But those evening shadows had been purple; these were a curious nigger brown. He remembered the cry "Come closer!" and then the terrible "I trusted you, you ——" followed by an obscenity and the downward crack of the whip. And now it was not he, but Stavro, who had been guilty of a betrayal.

Suddenly, as he walked through the archway, a voice hissed from the shadows: "*Kyrie! Kyrie!*"

It was the boy. But Patrick walked on.

"*Kyrie!* I want to tell you . . . I must speak to you . . . I want to . . ." Stavro was stumbling behind him over the rough cobbles.

The glare out in the roadway was cruel after the muted sunlight and shadow of the courtyard, but Patrick walked into it without any hesitation and crossed to the car.

"*Kyrie!*" the voice insisted.

He tugged open the door: "Sorry to keep you waiting. I couldn't find the camera at first."

"*Kyrie!*"

"What was Stavro trying to say to you?" Iris asked.

Patrick said: "Nothing I could possibly wish to hear." The car jerked forward.

"What are all these people doing?"

Mrs. Nicolidou roused herself and leant forward as they neared the centre of the town. Crowds were wandering up and down the streets, often six or seven abreast, and when Patrick sounded the horn or put out his head to shout, they would merely laugh and tell him to walk. Children kept jumping on the running-boards and the luggage-rack behind, and a young man in an exquisite suit of dove grey was marching beside them bawling out "It's a long way to Tipperary . . ." Everywhere outside the car there was laughter, shouting, colour: inside, the two women, morose and white-faced, had the appearance of cowering lower and lower, deeper and deeper, into the dusty and cracked leather upholstery.

"It's Easter Saturday," Mrs. Nicolidou said. "I'd forgotten about that. It's a great holiday. . . . Idiot," she muttered, as the young man in dove grey got the whole crowd to join in his song with him. "Oh, the idiot."

Far off a ship's hooter bellowed.

"Does that mean we've missed it?" Iris asked.

"Of course not. It must have only just berthed. You won't leave for hours." Mrs. Nicolidou touched Patrick's shoulder: "You're sure the young man will be there to drive me back!"

"Quite sure." She had already asked this question four times.

"I never thought you'd stay long. And I don't suppose you'll ever return."

"Of course we'll return," Iris said irritably. "Why shouldn't we return?"

"I knew you'd find life too dull for your sophisticated tastes. I didn't think it would work. You're both used to a world where things *happen*. They don't in Corfu."

Suddenly the street cleared: and the crowds which had milled round the car now pressed against each other under the arcades on either side. There was a curious, suspenseful silence such as one would hear in London during the war just before a flying-bomb exploded. A clock struck eleven, as Iris said:

"Look out! Draw up somewhere where we can shelter! Look out!"

As she spoke, there were yells, laughter and a crash and thud and clatter, as of blocks of masonry toppling into the roadway. Something hit the roof of the car; something else bounced off the bonnet. "What is it?" Patrick said. "What's happened?" He began to accelerate. "What are they trying to do?"

As the car screeched round a corner, Iris began to laugh weakly and hysterically, a handkerchief pressed to her mouth with the fingers of both hands as though she were attempting to staunch a wound.

"It's nothing," Mrs. Nicolidou said. "I'd forgotten about that. I should have warned you. It's one of the Easter customs. At eleven o'clock on Easter Saturday they chuck all their broken pots and pans out of the windows." She chuckled: "Did you think it was a revolution? Did you think they were going to lynch you—or stone you?" She had obviously enjoyed Patrick's bewilderment and fear.

They were now bumping down a side-street which sloped towards the harbour when door after door opened and groups of men and boys came out, laughing and shouting to each other and brandishing knives as they dragged a number of lambs out on to the cobbles. There was a pandemonium of rough voices, hob-nailed boots grating on stone, and the bleating of the animals which lay, shaking their heads and twitching convulsively, their feet tied, on either side of the road.

Iris put her hands to her eyes, but Mrs. Nicolidou stared from the window in stony contempt.

"Every year people say this thing must stop. And every year it happens. Oh, there's a cruelty in the Greek! We're a cruel people."

The car had to draw up where a small knot of people had congregated to watch an old man slaughter one of the lambs. The blood spurted over his hands and his boots and when, unselfconsciously, he patted his bristling white moustache, it too was dewed with drops that slowly shrivelled and darkened as they dried. Patrick looked with fascinated horror, first at the grinning face of the old man, then at the rapt faces of the onlookers, and finally at the knife with which the animal's skin was now being carefully peeled away. "Drive on," Iris said. "Why are you stopping? Drive on!"

"He can't drive on," Mrs. Nicolidou answered. "We're trapped."

Patrick sounded his horn repeatedly; then he put his head out of the window and began to shout. But the crowds, many of them couples whose hands were unselfconsciously linked as they gazed at the old man and his lamb, paid no attention. Like the skin of a fig the lamb's pelt was being deftly eased away to reveal the roseately glistening flesh beneath.

Suddenly Patrick leapt from the car. In a fury, he advanced on the crowds, shouting and gesticulating wildly, and at last pushing them by force to either side of the road. No one protested; no one resisted him. They were all laughing at the spectacle of the white-faced, trembling Englishman in his crumpled tropical suit and panama hat.

The car chugged on to an ironical clapping of hands and shouts of "Bravo!" Iris said: "That was horrible," and Mrs. Nicolidou replied, apparently forgetting her previous remark about the slaughtering: "Oh, you've become over-civilized! . . . Anyway, you must be used to blood, aren't you? It can't be anything new."

"It was horrible."

As they continued to bump down the hill towards the harbour, they passed other little groups gathered about other convulsively twitching lambs, until soon the gutters on either side were overflowing with blood streaked with dust and the cracks between the cobbles were saturated with it. The air seemed to have become heavy and moist, as though just before a thunderstorm, and everywhere there was a pervasive odour that made Patrick think of sawdust on tiled floors. He began to drive faster and faster, until Mrs. Nicolidou protested: "Do be careful! Do you want us to be slaughtered too?"

The white ship lay out in the bay at anchor; after what they had seen in the streets, both it and the water seemed to have about them an extraordinary cleanliness. Patrick felt the impulse to kneel down at the jetty and dip his hands over and over again into the waves; but he restrained himself.

They found the custom-house deserted and there was no motor-boat to take them out to the ship. A sleepy peasant-boy in a sailor's uniform, clumsily holding a rifle, told them that the custom's officer would be back, he did not know when; that there was no hurry, that the ship would not leave until evening. "Why don't you go over there and sit down and have a coffee? I'll call you when the officer arrives."

Once again Patrick lost his temper and he began to shout rudely about Greek inefficiency and the impossibility of living in such a country; at the end of which the sailor merely remarked, with an admirable dignity, that he was not himself a custom's officer but a harbour-guard. It was Easter, he added.

"Damn Easter!"

Patrick strode over to the Harbourmaster's office, and fortunately the Harbourmaster was there, not in his office, but in his own private quarters, where he and Dr. Petropoulos were drinking and listening to some scratchy gramophone records of *Parsifal*.

"But, my dear chap, are you leaving? I'd no idea. . . . We must see you off."

"No, really, it was just that I . . ."

"But of course we must see you off. Mustn't we, Petropoulos?"

"Of course."

The doctor swayed a little as he rose from his chair to turn off the gramophone.

"Of course, my dear chap. We shall go on board with you." He clapped his hands and shouted for his orderly to bring him his cap. "But, first, let me give you some whisky. I was brought this as a present by the captain of the American destroyer last week."

At first Patrick refused; then he swallowed the tumbler of whisky in three gulps.

When they reached the custom-shed, they found that the officer had returned and was already going through one of Iris's cases. The Harbourmaster called out: "All right, all right, Emmanouelides. That's all right! Let them through!" The sailor with the rifle was told to re-pack the articles that had already been taken out, but he performed this task so clumsily that Mrs. Nicolidou broke off from her conversation with Petropoulos to go over and scold him: "You're crushing everything! Leave it alone! Look what you have done to this dress!"

Although he usually had a strong head, the single tumbler of whisky had begun to make Patrick feel vaguely dizzy and somnolent. As he climbed into the motor-boat he tripped and fell sideways on to his mother-in-law, making the Harbourmaster and Petropoulos double over with high-pitched, cackling laughter: even the two sailors in charge giggled to each other. Everyone, except the two women, had drunk too much.

As the boat chugged out towards the steamer, Patrick looked back. The harbour-square lay dusty and deserted: there were two dogs, one scratching itself under a café table while the other stood and sniffed at it nervously; the sailor who had helped them; another sailor on duty outside the Harbourmaster's office; and a beggar asleep in the shadow of the chipped war memorial. Behind, the town rose, glittering level upon level, with here and there a jagged gap where a bomb had torn through, until, high up, the sky started, a curious peacock blue that was almost a mauve. The Harbourmaster, who had trained at Chatham, was saying: "It's a damned shame, old chap, that you should be leaving just now. This is when all the fun starts. You'll miss everything."

"Yes, you should stay until after Easter." Petropoulos agreed; he began to titter weakly, for no reason except that he was not used to drinking whisky.

A figure on a bicycle was shooting down the hill. It swerved to avoid a charabanc, bumped over the square, and then made full tilt for the jetty as though about to take off across the water. An arm waved; Patrick thought he could hear a shout.

He leant forward. He stared. And as he stared the boat began to veer, churning spray up on to his hands, his lips, and his dark glasses.

"Take care!" the Harbourmaster shouted. "Hold tight! You'll fall in!"

Again the figure waved; again Patrick thought he could hear that attenuated shout echoing across the water.

Then the boat passed behind the ship and he could see and hear no more.

They did not sail till late that evening. Iris went and lay down—she was tired, she said—while the rest of them drank and played bridge. Patrick always won: for though, with each drink he felt more and more confused about everything else, for the game alone his mind seemed to achieve a greater and greater clarity. Only occasionally he stumbled, and that was when, like some sudden surge of nausea, he would feel deep inside himself a memory revive of that figure waving and shouting on the quay while he himself looked back, gazing motionless through the spray that had spattered his dark glasses.

When, at last, all the members of the crew had returned and it was announced that they would sail in ten minutes, Patrick fetched Iris. She was standing at the port-hole, the late-evening light reflected off the waves on to her impassive face so that the skin gleamed with a curious luminosity. "Come and say good-bye," he said.

She turned and sighed: "Did you want to stay very much?" she asked. "Are you very sad at leaving?"

"No, of course not."

"You are." She came to him and put her arm through his, and then rested her cheek against his shoulder. "You're so kind to me," she said. "You were so happy there. And I've spoiled it all for you. But one day—one day I shall try to make it up. Somehow."

Petropoulos and the Harbourmaster who were by now extremely drunk, swayed and giggled and insisted on kissing both Patrick and Iris before they would descend the gangway. Mrs. Nicolidou said with a curious, offhand dryness: "When shall I see you both again? Never, I suppose."

"But we're only going away for two or three months," Patrick said.

"Oh, two or three months! You'll never return. I've told you, you're too sophisticated; not enough happens for you here. . . . No, I bet you that you'll never come back. Never!"

"Don't be silly, Mother! Don't talk like that!" Suddenly Iris was on the verge of tears. "Of course we shall return!"

Iris went below again as soon as the ship began to move, but Patrick stood on the deck, watching the night fall, fold on fold, about the receding island. The wind ruffled his hair and made his shirt flap against his chest, and his lips felt dry and tasted bitter and salty. For a time he could hear distant noise and a confused uproar of voices as the crowds surged, shouting and laughing, through the narrow alleys of the town. Then all that faded. He began to wonder why Stavro had bicycled down to the harbour, and what he was doing now. Perhaps he, too, was dancing with the crowds in the taverns. Perhaps he, too, was drunk. Anyway, they would never meet again. He and Soula would never meet again.

A rocket fizzed up into the sky and splintered into innumerable crimson roses that parted and dropped their petals, fading and gently dying, over the island. Another rocket followed. This time crimson petals lay like great drops of blood in the stifling folds of the night before a sudden tremor shook them spattering downwards.

A gong boomed out, reverberating across the water. A voice called: "Dinner, sir, Dinner."

7

AFTER the beauty of Corfu, Naples was horrible to them. Every day a wind rose soon after eleven to whirl dust down from the hills behind into the grease-grey sea. Everything tasted of dust, dust stung their eyes, even their pores seemed to sweat dust. Between the station and the hotel Iris's jewel-case was stolen and the apathy of the police exasperated her far more than the loss of the jewellery itself.

Why did they not leave? Patrick often asked himself the question. It seemed as if the compulsive impetus which had brought them, like migrating birds, across the fresh Adriatic to this squalid bay had spent itself, and now they lacked both the will and the energy to press on. Besides, they had never ceased to maintain to each other the pretence of having left Corfu merely for a holiday, and a certain speciousness was given to this lie by the act of spending large sums of money in a city of holiday-makers. Sometimes Patrick would say to Iris: "Tell me when you'd like to move," and she would reply: "You must see Pompei first," or: "You've still not visited Capri." Day after day he would go out on such expeditions, his camera slung about him, and he would never fail to look at every exhibit, enter every church, and listen to every word the guides spoke with a kind of sad stoical patience that never failed to win him the respect of his fellow-tourists. He was like a man who shams ill, he decided, and then, from some obscure motive of guilt, goes through all the ritual of being ill; taking his temperature, lying in bed, living on slops, dosing and injecting himself.

Iris, herself, never stirred except to take an occasional stroll at dusk up and down the sea-front. Their room had a balcony overlooking the bay and here she would lie in a wickerwork chair for hours on end, sometimes knitting, sometimes reading, but more often doing nothing at all. There was a terrible resigned sadness about her, but it no longer moved Patrick. He would watch her sometimes, when she did not know that she was being watched, and he would try to make himself pity her. She had become thin, her bones protruding unattractively; her hair was dull, as though thick with the dust that blew incessantly across the streets; the skin of her hands was flaky and peeling. She had lost all that large, voluptuous handsomeness that had once made people stare at her, wherever she went. But the more Patrick gazed, noting these changes, the less capable he became of feeling anything for her but a kind of exasperated resentment. And she, in turn, sensing his resentment, misinterpreted its cause: and a yet darker tinge was added to her moods of alternating depression and remorse.

One evening after dinner, which they had had brought up to them in their room, Patrick left her seated out in the balcony, innumerable moths clicking against her lamp as she read a detective novel, and wandered downstairs. He knew that if he stayed with her he would say something savage, if only to rouse her from that despairing stupor in which his life now passed. "For God's sake make an effort!" he would shout at her. "Do you think I'm not suffering? Do you?" And then he would taunt her with the whole ignominious story of Soula. . . . But would he? And he knew he would not. He would never give her that power over him, even though it might be the only thing to save her.

"A letter, sir."

It was his mother-in-law's writing but the letter was addressed to him. He was not surprised; it had been obvious all along that Mrs. Nicolidou preferred him to Iris, just as she always preferred men to women. As he placed the letter in his pocket and drifted out through the swing-doors into the cool April night, he felt a vague unease: he had thought he had severed all those threads that had tied him to the island, much as Petropoulos had severed the nerves about Christo's cancer in order to relieve intolerable pain; but now, shuttling across those hundreds of miles, there had come this light-blue rectangle and the invisible filament had already begun to throb.

He sat on a parapet above a rim of beach scurfy with twists of newspaper, bottles and tins, and tore the envelope open. There was a street-lamp beside him. A newspaper cutting fluttered downwards between his fingers and he had to stoop to retrieve it, the blood thumping disagreeably behind his eyes as he straightened once more. At first, without knowing it, he began to read the wrong side of the cutting. It was a story of a peasant who had learned that another peasant had been sleeping with his wife, and he and a band of his friends had gone to the rival's house in order to punish him; the rival was not there but his donkey was in the yard, and in the savagery of his rage, the peasant had put out the donkey's eyes. Why had Mrs. Nicolidou sent him this tale? Patrick wondered. She so often talked about the cruelty of the Greeks; perhaps she had wanted him to see this nauseating example of it. Once again he read through the laconic account, and he noticed, this time, that the man had been acquitted on condition that he gave his rival one of his own donkeys: he had, the judge said, acted under "intolerable provocation".

Then Patrick turned the cutting over. "Brother Kills Sister—Village Tragedy." Two middle-aged Americans passed and the man said: "Good evening" while the woman called over her shoulder: "I got my cameo—it's just like the one our friend got last year, you remember I told you." Patrick had sat next to them in the bus to

Positano that morning. Below, on the sand, a boy was walking, kicking at the tins and bottles that gleamed in the moonlight; his hands were in his pockets and his trousers were rolled up to the knee. ". . . found dying in the courtyard of a villa belonging to a Greek woman married to an Englishman. The weapon used was a sheath-knife . . . stabbed in twenty-seven different places . . . the assassin at once gave himself up to the police . . . girl pregnant . . ."

Shock after shock of pain screamed, incandescent, along that invisible filament; and then, as if the filament had all at once burned itself out, there was silence, darkness, deadness. A tin rattled hollow as the boy sent it spinning across the beach. A passing English voice said: "The last time I ate scampi I had hell for three days." A spiral of dust rose from the square.

Patrick got to his feet and still holding the envelope, the newspaper cutting and Mrs. Nicolidou's unread letter crumpled together in one fist, began to walk along the front. People stared at him, because he walked as if he were drunk, moving neither to right nor left to avoid the passers-by, his head sunk on his chest, and his feet dragging. He saw nothing, felt nothing, knew nothing: the whole world seemed to have become no more than an appalling ache at the back of the head, some paper in one hand, and a taste, thick and metallic, of dust on the tongue.

He had come to some gardens and he wandered through their shadows, as slowly, nerve by throbbing nerve, sensation returned. First there was a terrible nausea, when he clung to a tree and thought he was going to vomit; then there was a no less terrible grief; and then there was a baffled agony in which he asked himself over and over again—Why? Why? Why? Like bits of broken glass, fragments of the past rasped together somewhere deep within him, tearing him as they did so: Dino whipping Stavro while Soula looked on; Soula's hand in his at the cinema; Stavro pointing out his Danish friend on the blotched photograph; Stavro dripping with rain after his bicycle ride to town to fetch the printing-paper; Soula clutching him in the darkroom; pebbles cascading down the rock upon their locked bodies; a figure shouting and waving on a deserted quay; a rocket bursting. . . .

He sank on to a stone bench and put his head in his hands.

Why? Why? Why? And Soula had been pregnant. Had Stavro known that? And who was the father? The cadet-officer perhaps. And in that case . . . But he could not understand it.

Someone had sat down beside him. "Excuse me, Joe—got a light?"

Of course Greeks had a fanatical sense of honour, of family honour. In the courtyard . . . the knife . . . he knew that knife. . . . In the dusk a boy was throwing it against a tree, throwing it and retrieving it, throwing it and retrieving it. It was a present, a present from a Danish sailor.

"Joe . . . a light . . . got a light?"

The face was youthful yet predatory; something simian about the nostrils and the over-wide grin. A hand which was almost a claw gripped Patrick's wrist as he held out the lit match. "Thanks, Joe."

A barefooted girl was arguing with two sailors under a tree, until suddenly one lunged at her. They struggled and she broke free, shying off into the darkness with a strange high-pitched cackling. The boy puffing his cigarette beside Patrick said: "Whore." He drew one knee up.

Along an ochre beach two children ran, the boy chasing the girl, until he caught her, put his arms round her and carried her into the water. They were beautiful, how beautiful. The memory of them blew through the close, teeming garden like some sudden whiff of the distant sea across a stagnant marsh. Beautiful, innocent, savage. The words rose up inside him like the sobs which hung somewhere in his throat, choking him yet refusing to break out.

Why? Why? Why?

He got up and wandered on, deeper and deeper into the gardens. All round him shadows quivered; leaves rustled; voices whispered. He turned and saw that the young man who had asked him for a cigarette was pattering behind. The youth overtook him, looked over his shoulder and gave his simian grin. Then he walked on, with an exaggerated litheness, stopped by a tree and waited.

"Pssst! . . . Joe! . . . Pssst!"

As Patrick passed, the extraordinary cat-like hiss followed along behind him.

And suddenly he understood: he understood it all.

8

It was seven weeks later that the package arrived; posts from Greece are always sluggish and in this case a further delay had no doubt been caused by the illegibility of the handwriting, like some obscure cuneiform, in which it had been addressed.

Patrick had been out riding before breakfast, and when he got back, Iris had already gone, he supposed to one of those almost daily committee meetings from which she would return exhausted and pale and yet with that subdued elation which now seemed to come to her whenever she had successfully exerted her personal power over those about her. For a few days after their return from Italy her mood of resigned melancholy had remained; then, with what was obviously a heroic gathering of her forces, she had thrown herself into a life which was as close as possible in pattern to the life she had lived in Corfu. In that routine of impersonal service to people for whom she seemed to feel little pity and no affection, she had found the most effective of anodynes. Patrick marvelled at her recovery; and yet he was appalled. It seemed as if the healing of that terrible emotional wound had resulted in a tough mass of scar tissue, through which it was now impossible to pass to whatever tenderness lay sealed beneath. Patrick remembered how when they had first arrived in Corfu, he had been astonished at how like her mother Iris seemed, when she told Christo and his two helpers where to place their luggage; her voice taking on the same authoritative edge and her hands the same authoritative gestures. Yet now that resemblance seemed to have grown even more marked.

It had been a beautiful morning: he had ridden out in a mist that clung, soft and thick, to the gentle contours of the slopes about the house, but as the sun rose, so the mist rose with it, seeming to disintegrate in the branches of the trees on which the first leaves huddled. He felt well, he felt happy as he stopped on the brow of the hill above the house and looked back, letting the reins drop slack so that the horse could crop grass. The Swiss maid was laying the breakfast and he could see her blonde hair as from time to time it caught the sunlight that was now streaming through the window of the morning-room. On the terrace one of the dogs was scratching itself. The workmen had already arrived to repair the roof, and were stacking their bicycles in the yard and fetching out their ladders. It was his, all his: and he felt it, like a bandage, wrapped gently, gently in an endless cocoon about him, muffling all shocks from without or stirrings from within.

Hours would now pass during which he never thought of Corfu, of Soula or of Stavro. His life, he sometimes told himself, had become like the lake: stagnant, it was true, yet not unbeautiful in that stagnation, except when sudden winds tore at the surface, as though (he was obsessed with that image) some surgical instrument were pushing away the cataract-like membrane from the living eye. The sudden pungency of an orange he was peeling in his hands; the glimpse of a boy from the farm standing at the end of a lane at evening; a girl's laughter heard from the distant road; the click of his camera-shutter . . . Momentarily the instrument would jab. But for the most part, he now was forgetting; he was putting it all away from him, as all his life he had put away whatever he felt might cause him discomfort or pain. Stavro, he had heard, had been sent to a reformatory; and sometimes Patrick tried to imagine what kind of love it could have been that drove him to commit that horrible, useless act of violence. What kind of love? . . . And he had never guessed—had never suspected! But at this point his mind would let go of it all; would let go, would turn elsewhere, would forget. The bandage would slip back to cover up the place.

Yet here was this package: with the Greek stamp, his name and address written out in that curious cuneiform, and on the back the name of the sender in Greek.

It was not more than a brown envelope, and inside, wrapped in a sheet from an old copy of *The Times*, lay that pair of dark glasses he had once given to Soula. One of the lenses was shattered, perhaps in the post or perhaps—Patrick experienced a terrible nausea as the thought came to him—in some struggle, that last struggle even, between the two children. He stared down at the glittering scars that clung like a delicate encrustation of frost to the oval glass; then he stared out through the window at the beautiful spring landscape—at the terrace on which the dog now slept, at the garden beyond it, at the fields, at the hills, at the lucent curve of the sky. He raised the glasses to his eyes; slowly he put them on, crossed to the french windows and, resting his hands on the jambs on either side, once more gazed out.

Through the broken lens the whole scene itself looked broken, cracks reaching hither and thither over its entire surface. It was a new world he saw, and yet it was still that old world, serene and sunlit, at which he had been staring only a minute or two ago. The sky was now a horrible livid colour; the hills, humped grey beneath it looked as impenetrably dense as rocks; the leaves on the young trees were sere; the pathway leading down to the woods seemed to rush, precipitous and dark, like some swollen torrent; the first roses in the garden had turned a purple that was almost jet. And everywhere the flaws ran like intricate nerves carrying their messages of shock, grief, agony.

He continued to stare, bewildered, thrilled and, in some extraordinary way, strengthened by the terrible, morbid beauty of this world as it had at last been revealed to him.

He knew now that he would always see it like that. It would never change.

ALSO AVAILABLE FROM VALANCOURT BOOKS

Lightning Source UK Ltd.
Milton Keynes UK
UKOW04f1315081214

242825UK00002B/76/P